The Men We Make

The Men
We Make

Magnus Johnson

This book may be purchased for educational, business or sales promotional use. For permission requests, contact:

BorneWilder Attn: Sara Johnson, Permissions Email:: Sara@bornewilder. com

Copyright © 2025 by BorneWilder & Magnus Johnson. All rights reserved. Published by BorneWilder

Book cover design by Sara Johnson

First Edition, 2025

ISBN 979 8 90148 736 5

To My Wife

Who didn't tell me my writing was good until it was.

Forward

It was my pleasure to meet Magnus when he was an under-graduate student at George Fox University in Oregon. Our relationship began in the classroom, where I served as his primary professor and advisor. We connected immediately as military veterans. I served aboard a nuclear ballistic missile submarine and later on an aircraft carrier, and Magnus served three combat tours as a United States Army Green Beret. That shared experience, combined with our mutual love for psychology and human healing, became the beginning of a friendship that will last a lifetime.

Magnus is also a devoted husband and father. His commitment to learning has shaped every stage of his life. After completing his undergraduate degree, he pursued graduate studies in psychology, counseling, and coaching. He is a voracious reader, a sought-after speaker, an engaged author, and a great American hero. I am honored to write this foreword because in *The Men We Make*, Magnus draws on his deep understanding of human behavior, human development, and the forces that shape our attachments to explore two possible paths in the life of the central character, Darin. To say much more would diminish the experience of discovery that awaits you in these pages. What I can say is this. Once you have reflected on the story, you will find yourself making more intentional and effective choices in your own life as an adult, a spouse, and a parent. We learned long ago how the art and science of nurturing relationships shape our attachments to one another. As we reflect on those attachments across the lifespan, we begin to see how profoundly they influence the generations that follow. These patterns do not always form the way they should, and that is why we must remain lifelong learners, continually growing in the wisdom needed to guide those who depend on us.

In 2013 Magnus launched Mission 22, a nonprofit organization created to provide healing and support for military veterans facing Post Traumatic Stress and the risk of suicide. At that time the VA estimated that twenty-two veterans died by suicide every day. Mission 22 has grown into a national organization that raises awareness and provides innovative physical and mental wellness programs for veterans who have experienced Post Traumatic Stress, Military Sexual Trauma, non-deployable injuries, and for the families who stand beside them. All services are provided at no cost. The organization now supports about 2600 participants each year and reaches hundreds of thousands more through its national outreach. There are many reasons for its success, but one key factor is that Magnus and those who share his vision are lifelong learners. Real learning is not a degree or a project. It is a mindset. It is a way of showing up for others. I consider myself a lifelong learner as well. Over the past fifty years I have earned six graduate degrees, including two doctorates, and worked in ten medical and psychiatric hospitals. I have taught across several academic programs at six universities. I know psychology in both theory and practice. Yet I can say without hesitation that the servant leadership Magnus brings to this work is extraordinary.

Families shape their children, and Magnus takes that truth further by showing how experience shapes the adults those children become. In Darin's story he reveals how the connections within dysfunctional families are formed, supported, and repeated over time. You will see how the foundation of dysfunction can echo across generations. This book will help you make sense of your own life. Magnus shows how the stories families live by, both spoken and unspoken, teach us how to understand reality. These stories tell us who we are, how we communicate, what we fear, what helps us survive, and what happens when the conditions around us suddenly change or refuse to change at all. This novel will leave you with many powerful "What if?" questions. It will also invite reflection through the dialogues between the characters and the dialogue you will inevitably have within yourself. If you do not see ways this story applies to your own life, then something in your story has yet to be understood. Once you finish this book, you will likely feel a deep compassion for Darin, for others like him, and perhaps even for yourself. After all, we must all ask at some point who made us, and who we are making in return.

The Men We Make will help you understand your own life mor clearly. It will also help you understand the people around you.

Dr. Carl Lloyd, PhD, PsyD, LPC, MAC
Tenured Professor, Emeritus, George Fox University

Preface

The Men We Make is meant to make the reader uncomfortable; the same world written in two ways is to show the reader that it matters how hard they try to be better, not perfect. A man trying to be sober is better than a drunk who thinks they don't need help. An overbearing aunt who is heavy-handed with religion is better than one who is a domineering junkie who abuses her family without remorse. In this novel, no character is without blemish and flaws; the only difference is that in part one, they don't give a damn, and in part two, they try their best even if it's in vain. Sometimes, even a misguided effort is enough to save ourselves and the ones we love.

Part two of the novel reimagines Part One. I have often wondered how my life would have been different if I had made other choices. In my literary work, I explored how a child's life would be different if the people in their lives made different choices. We all have distinct personalities; some of us are people pleasers, and others are inherently selfish. It is not our nature alone that impacts those in our lives, but rather how we choose to influence our environment by our actions.

Before printing my novel, I shared the story with people I respect who would offer me honest, productive criticism. Almost all of them said that the first part of the novel was emotionally hard to read. I was ecstatic; I wanted the readers to experience isolation and depersonalization. However, most confessed that they had struggled only through the first part of the novel because I had promised them that the anguish of the reading experience was worth the price. In part two of the novel, the readers felt relief. That is because I alter the context of the experience by changing the nature of the supporting characters.

For example, the matriarch Donna is a controlling, domineering figure in both parts one and two. However, in Part Two, the character is tempered by Christianity and by her husband. In part, one of Darin's relatives, Marty, is a person with alcoholism who has no intention of controlling his drinking or behavior. Whereas in part two, Marty attends an Alcoholics Anonymous meeting and is trying his best to be a sober man. Their nature is the same, but the choices they make to better themselves protect their family and themselves from the outside world.

All of us impact others' lives. Every frown, harsh word, or flippant interaction is contributing to the demise of our fellows. Yet we can choose to listen more attentively, pray more, and hope longer if we wish to protect ourselves and our communities from evil. I wrote this novel to remind good people that their efforts to do right, even if they go unrewarded, are desperately needed in this world. The book is meant to give hope to those readers who are starting to crumble under the weight of a world they inherited. I wish to show them that reality can be different if they escape or grow out of a toxic family dynamic.

Yes, part one of my book is a challenging read, but the relief of part two would be impossible to experience without the reader first enduring the darkness. A warm fire is valued much more when we come into a house from the cold. Just as a meal satisfies us if we haven't eaten all day. We sometimes need to feel the absence of love to understand its actual value. I hope my readers come away with a sense of relief that their lives are not as bad as they thought, and with a new humility and appreciation for the people in their lives who are trying, even if their efforts are imperfect.

Magnus Johnson

The Men We Make

Part 1

For the wages of sin is death, but the free gift of God is
eternal life in Christ Jesus our Lord.

-Romans 6:23

Chapter 1

The rain never stops when a man is close to murder. Incessant downpour, overcast, lonely. Days of rain drive men to madness. Perhaps it's the lack of vitamin D or the prolonged periods of isolation. Either way, men with pain find it harder to withstand suffering during a wet season. Such was the case with Darin, a landscape laborer, on the edge of desolation.

He lived in the basement of his mother's sister. She was white trash, but as with all matriarchs of the underworld, she didn't care. She made her living by having large garage sales and furnishing broken homes with recycled furniture and cheap keepsakes. Donna was tall for a woman who wore tight jeans and 80's rock band shirts with the sleeves cut off. She smoked Virginia Slims because they were classy and economical.

Donna always made breakfast for Darin—two fried eggs on toasted wonder bread. "Darin!" She yelled from the kitchen. "Breakfast is ready." Darin never raised his voice; he was not the kind of man who needed to acknowledge that he had heard someone speak to him.

His room in the basement of Donna's house was bare. He had a small mattress, sheet-less and placed directly on the floor. The walls were surrounded by cheap, veneer paneling installed by Donna the day before Darin moved in.

Every morning for months, he had hoped that the rain would cease at night. He dimly wished for a reprieve of his torture. The thought that he could move away from Portland never came to him. He could see the moisture and dampness in his dingy room with a basement window full of spider webs. He suffered under an oppressive layer of humidity intermixed with mold. He turned on his lamp which had no shade.

His body was pale but powerful; abuse and toil had shaped his form. He slept only in his tighty-whities that were neither white nor tight. Next to his bed were his pants, boots, and Jans Sport hoodie. He put on his clothes, which were still moist from yesterday, and went upstairs. At the kitchen table Donna sat smoking a cigarette. She had an air of regalness despite her poverty. The pressing matters of the ensuing day were weighing on her. The tension in her body meant that she would need Darin somehow.

He sat down without saying a word and began to eat. No salt or pepper was needed; just margarine and ketchup were placed on the table with the food.

"What time do you think you'll get off work today?" She asked.

Darin hated this ritual almost as much as the rain.

"I dunno," he replied without eye contact. He never could find a way to escape his bondage to Donna. He was too simple, too broken to imagine a different life, let alone create one.

"I want your help when you get back getting that dresser out

of the basement. I got a buyer from Lake Oswego that wants it bad."
Donna always had a prospective buyer coming in, flush with cash and
ready to be hustled. She would have been a successful merchant under
different circumstances.

"Okay," he responded as he was finishing off the last of the toast.

"Don't be late again, Darin, or I'll tell Marty you can't work for
him anymore."

Pulling his hood up in preparation for stepping into the rain,
Darin agreed.

He waited for Marty under the clear, green awning of the
porch. The man he worked for was an alcoholic who had spent several
years on and off in prison. Marty was always starting and stopping
landscaping companies to avoid paying his debts to subcontractors
and homeowners who were unimpressed with his work. All of these
companies always had his name in them. Marty's Yard Care, Marty's
Landscaping, and Design of Nature by Marty. He was an arrogant
liar, somehow related to Darin and Donna. Darin had no idea how
they shared blood, but he accepted it.

The white work truck pulled into the driveway with a new logo
on the door panels: Marty's Landscapes.

"Hop in boy! We got ourselves a big contract!" Marty hollered
from the driver's seat.

Darin lumbered down the porch stairs. He didn't want to go
with Marty, but he didn't want to be in the rain anymore. The door
stuck on the first pull but opened on the second jerk. Darin got in and
looked at Marty.

"Always the same shit with you, Darin. How's about a 'Good
Morning' or a 'Hell yeah!'"

"Good morning, Marty," Darin said softly and flatly.

"Gooood mooorning, mother fucker!" said Marty as he fished out another camel cigarette and lit it with his Zippo lighter. Marty then closed the lighter with a flick of his wrist that could only be acquired by years of smoking; he put the truck in reverse with flare.

It was a short drive from Oregon City to Lake Oswego. Darin's thoughts seemed to prolong the trip. Marty continued to talk, unaware or not concerned that Darin was not listening and barely pretended that he was. Darin slouched against the door without his seat belt. His face rested on the window. As they commuted, the rain began to turn into a mist, and the gray settled in.

The property they would work on was one of those houses where the buyer removes everything. There is the sort of people that settle into what already exists and there is the sort that reinvents their habitat. Darin knew immediately that this property was owned by people who had the means and the entitled ability to buy a property with a vision to reconstruct it in their own image. Darin was disappointed, but he did not place much value in his thoughts.

Marty smashed his cigarette in the overflowing ashtray. After getting out of the truck, Darin finished putting it out. Marty went to the front door and knocked. Within a few moments, a woman answered. She was tall with wavy black hair, confident, and slightly annoyed to be summoned. Marty and the woman exchanged a few words, and then she shut the door. Marty turned to face the truck and waved Darin to come. Darin got out of the vehicle and approached Marty. Marty waited with forced patience for Darin to come to him. "Grab the pry bars and hammers. We will rip out the fence in the backyard."

Darin turned and rummaged through the bed of the truck for

the tools. He grabbed them and followed Marty around to the side of the house. Marty was looking at a wood gate that had deteriorated prematurely due to the Pacific Northwest moisture.

"Start taking this gate down," Marty said.

Darin nodded and started prying out the nails with his cat's paw and hammer. Marty watched him for a moment and commented that he should save any boards he could because he might be able to sell them. Darin worked on the gate with focus until he noticed movement out of the corner of his eye. He turned to identify the movement and realized that it was the woman. A window by the gate made it possible for him to see her in the kitchen.

She moved with feminine elegance. Her wavy hair almost reached the back pockets of her Levi's. She was beautiful, and Darin was entranced. The woman, who was watering her plants, seemed to be coaxing them to flourish by leaning near them.

"Hey!" Marty shouted. "What are you doing?"

"Nothing," said Darin.

Startled by the shock of being forcefully awakened from his trance, Darin composed himself and returned to work. He glanced over his shoulder and saw that Marty was gone. Darin then peeked back at the window to see if the woman was alarmed. He locked eyes with her. Darin realized that she was looking because of Marty's yelling. He broke her gaze and shrunk back to his task. Feeling her eyes still locked on him, he kneeled and started pulling the nearby nails.

As he worked, he started to imagine that this woman was his. He let his mind wander. The power of her presence and the lack of passion in his life created a storm of lust and fantastical musings. As he pulled boards, his focus was on that gaze. Did she want him? Was that visual exchange proof of her desire? The work moved quickly once he got a rhythm going. At around 4 o'clock, Marty appeared. Darin was about halfway finished with the fence, and he could tell that Marty was impressed.

"You got to work faster if you want me to keep paying you," Marty said as he got nearer.

Darin just looked at him.

"You know, I try to help you out because Donna asked me to keep an eye out for ya."

"I know," said Darin.

"Well, let's start wrapping up for the day," Marty said as he walked off.

Darin looked around and tried to understand what Marty wanted cleaned up, but there was no mess. Darin had kept the area organized while he worked, and there was nothing to "wrap up." He put his tools in his belt and headed for the truck. As he rounded the corner of the house, he saw Marty and the woman talking at the front door. Marty was stretching his posture like a bird puffing and dancing to attract a mate. The woman was not responsive to his masculine exaggerations. As she spoke to him, she looked over his shoulder and set her soft eyes on Darin.

Immediately, Darin was uncomfortable but held her gentle stare. Then she returned her eyes to Marty and finished speaking. A few moments later, they ended the exchange, and Marty turned to the truck. His face was contorted with anger.

"Get in the truck," Marty said with a hiss of rage.

Darin threw his tools in the back and got in the truck.

"What the fuck are you doing?" Marty exploded when the truck doors were shut, and the engine was running. "Melissa said that you were staring at her through the window this morning, making her uncomfortable. What the hell are you doing, you damned creep? Just do your fucking job and stop being a shitbag creeper."

A torrent of anxiety flushed Darin. He couldn't believe that she said this to Marty. He thought they had a moment of connection.

Darin started to respond, but Marty cut him off.

"I told her you were simple and didn't mean nothin' by it."

"I didn't mean nothin', Marty," Darin said.

"Keep your eyes to yourself tomorrow, you understand?" Marty inquired.

"I will; I will keep my eyes to myself tomorrow," said Darin.

With that, Marty lit a cigarette and backed out of the driveway. The workday was over.

Chapter 2

There is an order to our design. When it is not followed, there is sure to be suffering and shame. We cannot escape the flesh, but it can be disciplined. Fathers cause families to corrupt themselves by their tyranny or their absence. Darin grew up with no father. He was alone in the world, except for his mother's sister. Donna was the only shelter and source of stability Darin had known in his short life. That shelter came at a price, and the fee was shameful.

When Darin got out of Marty's truck and shut the door, Marty immediately and aggressively backed out of the driveway. Darin observed the hazardous maneuver Marty commanded with his truck. There was some glimmer of hope that a trash truck would smash into Marty, killing him instantly. However, the simple and the wicked seem to be protected to torment the weak. Marty backed onto the road without paying attention to traffic and then sped off.

Donna's house had a large driveway with stairs leading to the second level. Pausing to look at the home, Darin hesitated to go inside. Today was Friday, and he knew that Donna would be drunk.

The desire to rest and reenter familiarity can beacon a tormented soul back to a source of its anguish despite revulsion. Darin lumbered up the stairs. The rain continued to drown out clarity in his mind. The stairs were covered by sea green corrugated roofing paneling

At the door, Darin paused. He did not want to enter, but he was cold and hungry. He looked through the door's window and observed Donna cooking, dancing, and smoking. She was drunk and not alone. On the couch was Shannon, she was yet another person Donna used but pretended to befriend. They were laughing and gesturing to the music. Darin entered, and both women swooned with intoxication.

"Hey, baby!" Donna said as she swayed her ample hips.

Shannon cackled and took a long drag off her cigarette as she roused herself to focus on him. She smiled, and Darin blushed and became aggravated because of sensing Donna's jealousy.

"Best mind your manners, Shannon," she said with maternal covetousness.

Shannon lay back on the couch and took another drag off her cigarette. "I just think he's cute, Donna; not going to bite him," Shannon said as she gazed at Darin with a lustful invitation.

"Come here and kiss your aunt, Darin," Donna insisted with false concern. "You are all wet and looking tired. Dinner will be ready soon, and then we will have a good time."

Darin did as he was asked. Donna reached her arms around him and pressed herself against him. He was aroused and embarrassed because Shannon was watching.

"Get yourself cleaned up and then come eat, hon," Donna said with controlling confidence. "Okay," Darin said, waiting for her to release him. When she did, he turned to head toward the stairs leading to his bedroom. As he moved across the living room, he watched Shannon through his peripheral vision and admired her. She was tall, thin, younger than Donna, and wore revealing clothing. He wanted her but knew that Donna would never allow it.

The shower in the basement was covered in mildew. Darin had a bar of Irish Spring soap and a bottle of Head & Shoulders shampoo and conditioner. The water was always too hot or too cold; he could never adjust the heat to a comfortable temperature. When Darin got out of the shower, he dried himself off with a stained white towel. Before exiting the shower, he locked eyes with himself in the mirror.

His own face seemed foreign and hostile. He was looking at an animation that he was unfamiliar with. He gazed with curiosity and stillness at his own reflection, peering into his own eyes, looking for something. He searched the windows to his soul and found only a stranger looking back. Every time he saw his own reflection, he would look for something, and, every time, he would abandon the search unfulfilled.

Darin put on his clean Dickies and white undershirt and went to his bed and lay down to wait. Donna would forget him until dinner was ready, and she may even forget him altogether if other men had been invited to drink. Lying on his sheetless mattress on the floor, lit by a shadeless lamp, he waited. Sleep overtook him, and he was awakened by Shannon who drunkenly roused him.

She pulled down his pants and put her mouth on him. He lost control almost instantly, and Shannon became rigid by the unexpected shock.

"What the fuck?" Shannon said with disgust as she spit on

his blanket. Darin was flooded with embarrassment and began pulling up his pants. Bewildered, Shannon got up to leave, as Donna opened the door.

"What's going on here?" Donna said in a flat tone.

Jimmy was behind Donna, laughing and echoing his lover. "Yeah, what's going on," he said mockingly.

"Shannon was trying to wake me up to drink with you guys," Darin blurted. Appeased with his answer, Donna and Jimmy left to go back upstairs. Shannon looked at Darin and laughed. Her eyes were barely open, and she still had a bit of a mess on her face. As she left, Darin pulled his pants up and rolled over. He had never had contact with any woman except Donna. He was flooded with guilt, curiosity, and embarrassment.

"Don't ever do that again," she said as she stumbled to her feet and out of his room, wiping her face with her shirt. Darin said nothing as she left. He pretended to go back to sleep. He spent the rest of the night listening to the sound of drunkards, hoping that they would remain upstairs and fearing that they wouldn't.

If Donna had a man for the night, Darin would not have to sleep with her. Jimmy was a neighborhood drunk and was often Donna's willing lover. Sometimes, Jimmy would be locked up or gone on a bender for weeks. In those periods, Donna would relentlessly have Darin in her bed. She was a lustful woman, and she had been having Darin please her since he came to stay after his mother had died.

As Darin drifted off to sleep, he noticed that the dresser Donna wanted to sell today was still in his room. He had agreed to be home to help her bring it out for the buyer. She must have sold something else, Darin thought. He had emptied all his belongings from the dresser as she had commanded. Nothing was his. Everything was transient and ethereal.

Not even his own body and eyes were his. They belonged to something else, someone else. He was in a home that was not his, a world that pushed him along without agreement or invitation. Adrift, alone, and used. Darin was not a man but a manifestation or a residue of others. Rage was building in him, and he had no one to blame. It just was. There was only pain, only distance.

Darin woke up and headed upstairs for food. The remnant of debauchery was everywhere. Women's undergarments were strewn about; empty bottles and ashtrays were heaped with cigarette butts. Shannon was on the couch with an unknown man. Her eyeliner was smeared, and she looked older in the morning light than she appeared yesterday.

Darin grabbed bread off the counter and headed outside. The morning was damp, and the air was heavy. Birds were busy with their bustle of chores. Stellar jays alarmed and robins hopped. Eating bread but wishing for eggs, Darin consumed the filler with dissatisfaction. He knew that Donna would not be up for hours, and that even when she did rise, she might still be drunk. He had learned long ago not to hope or wish.

Darin went back into the house, and the scene was the same. Wasting no time, Darin returned to his bedroom to get dressed. He put on the clothes he had worn yesterday and left the house. He would walk for hours. Not to a destination but for the sake of movement. To be still while awake was unsettling and left him feeling weak and disjointed. The weekends were difficult for Darin. He always woke early, but there was nothing to do. Donna would be sleeping or drunk, and

Marty rarely wanted to work over the weekends.

Darin wore wolverine boots that Marty had given him as hand-me-downs. They were too large, and he would have to over-tighten his shoes to keep them on his feet. Oversized footwear added disproportion to Darin's already strange countenance. Muscular but hunched, wearing dirty and oversized work apparel, Darin looked like an aged worker from his last job. Despite his demeanor, Darin was powerful, and walking several hours was not unusual for him.

After a few minutes of walking, the rain started, and Darin pulled up his hood and drew the drawstrings. His boots began to make squishing sounds as he trundled along. On his left was a 7-Eleven, where his mother occasionally bought fruit pies for him. He remembered liking the berry pies best, but, usually, only apple were available.

The last time they were at this 7-Eleven, she had gotten him an apple pie. He knew there was something wrong, but he did not realize that she was going to die. The doctors had told Donna that Darin's mother was very sick because of alcoholism and anorexia. Donna did not seem to understand that a person could die from drinking. Perhaps she was right, and Darin's mother died of some other disease not yet discovered by the medical professionals.

Donna explained to Darin that his mother was very sick, and that they would have to take good care of her. They cared for her by drinking more beer than and letting her eat whatever she wanted. Donna said his mother would be okay if they just "took good care," and he believed her. Darin would fetch her beer and cigarettes whenever she asked him to help her get better. The last day they left the house, Darin's mother said she would get him berry pie if he would help her get something to drink at the 7-Eleven.

Darin did precisely that. He guided her steps and helped steady her walk to the convenience store. On the way, he was lost in thought of the berry pie being there. He even expressed his hope to his mother, who was clammy and weak. With her pale face and shaking hands, she said, "Wish in one and shit in the other and see which hand fills up faster."

Darin understood what she meant, but he did not give up hope, and he kept his desires to himself for the rest of the journey. When they got to the store, Darin's mother seemed to regain strength as she rushed to the back. He went to the counter and saw no berry pies, and he asked the clerk if he had any in the back. The employee just shook his head and stood in place with his eyes watching Darin's mother.

His mom had gotten her liquor, and she placed the bottles on the counter. Darin grabbed an apple pie and put it next to the alcohol.

"See, boy?" Darin's mother said. "Hope is a waste of time."

Darin looked at her and said nothing. His eyes swelled with tears. His emotions were swirling, and he had no words.

The wasting woman glared at her son and hissed, "Don't waste your time on hope and believe nothing you hear and only half of what you see."

Darin wiped away his tears. His mother paid for the whiskey and opened a bottle as soon as they left the store. Her color returned, and on the walk home Darin got no assurance.

He had failed to listen to his mother's words and hoped again that she would be okay, and things would be as they used to be. When they got home, she sent Darin outside to play, and when he returned home before dark, he found her dead. His mother was right. There was no hope. Her lifeless body was rigid and pale.

Chapter 3

Darin reached below the berry pies, clutched an apple one in his hand, placed it on the counter, paid, and left the store. Marty paid Donna directly whatever income Darin had earned working for him. She would always have a reason not to give Darin his full pay. This month, there was a need to buy more groceries due to Darin's over-eating. She had given him money but only a fifty-dollar bill. Darin was unsure how much money he had made, but fifty was enough to cover his expenses.

He instinctively headed in the opposite direction of his home. The rain had soaked through his hoodie, but he was not cold. He traveled to his bridge where he could stay dry and eat his apple pie. Parks were strange. From a distance, they looked inviting and clean. Perhaps parks in other places and times were for children and their mothers. Darin's bridge and park were not clean nor inviting once he was off the trail. Bums loitered around, coming down off drugs, raved insanely, or stared with murderous intent.

Darin was uninterested in these feral men because he knew

that they were predators and addicts that were insane. Men who were depraved, alone, and empty comforted him by their lack of illusion. He had first discovered this bridge many years ago.

He remembered a time that Donna had asked him to clean the kitchen. She had only given him a dirty rag and told him to have it spotless when she got home.

He worked diligently and made the kitchen as clean has he could without soap, brushes or clean towels. Donna got home around 3:00 a.m. and woke him. He sat up in his bed and rubbed his eyes. When he locked eyes with Donna, she seemed strange, contorted, empty, and sinister.

"Didn't I tell you to clean the kitchen?" Donna hissed.

"I did...I did just like you told me to," Darin responded.

"You need to learn how to clean and finish what you start," Donna whispered as her eyes narrowed on him.

Darin was dumbfounded. He waited. Did he clean everything? he wondered. After a few moments, Donna stood and took off her clothes. She was large. Her breasts were scarred, and they sagged. Her hips and buttocks expanded once her jeans were off. She then got into his bed and told him she would teach him to finish a job.

She straddled his face and told him to clean his mouth. He was in shock and did not know what she meant. He had an erection, but he was terrified. Donna grew more carnal and started to grind her pelvis on his face.

"Lick it," she said, undulating.

Darin did as he was told, and her movements grew in pressure and pace. Her smell was putrid. He had never smelled anything like it, and it made him sick as he performed. After she was done, she crawled on all fours and told Darin to "put that prick in me." Darin had no idea what she meant, but she backed up and started to grind on his erection; with her hand, she inserted Darin into her. She did the work, and Darin was frozen in shock. Somehow, his body was engaged in this act of sex while his consciousness reeled in revolt. He lost control and experienced his first orgasm.

Donna got up and dressed. Standing above him and glaring she said, "If you can't do your work, you'll have to earn your room and board in bed." She left his room, and Darin lay there motionless. His thoughts raced. What had just happened? Was the kitchen not clean enough? Would this happen again?

He couldn't sleep the rest of the night and left the house searching for escape. He instinctively headed to the park where his mother used to take him. Shame drove him off the paths, and he discovered the bridge. Seeking the shadows, he sprinted up the concrete ramp and curled up in the darkness of the abutment. It was damp, dark, and concrete, but it was true.

The other men who sought out this bridge were a threat to people who did not belong but instinctively knew their own kind. Darin was unafraid, and they suffered their demons without coming near Darin. This world was inhabited by the dying, the sick, and the unloved. It was a refuge for men who had no home, no control, no purpose.

He ascended to his cave under the bridge and opened his pie. Each bite gave him vague comfort. This world was his; this food was his; and he relished both. Once he was finished with the snack, he placed the wrapper behind the concrete where his other wrappers were. He did not like carrying trash with him. He also despised full pockets. Any time he received change, he would leave it for the children with cancer on the counter of the 7-Eleven.

After eating, Darin would sit for hours listening to subterranean sounds of traffic muffled by the bridge. At first, there would be a jolt, then a hum, followed by another and another. This rhythmic sound and vibration would soothe Darin, and often he would nap. Today was no different, and Darin drifted off, entranced by the incessant sensation of motion and weight bearing.

He was startled awake by laughter, the kind only minions of hell could muster. When his eyes adjusted, he noticed a faint glow and knew the tramps had a barrel fire going. It must be late, he thought to himself. Darin slid deftly out of his crevice with little more than the slight sound of fabric against concrete.

As he moved home, the sun started to set, and he hurried out of habit more than fear. Reaching his driveway, Darin was relieved that no lights were on. He quickly pounced up the steps and twisted the doorknob to enter. He got into bed and turned off the lamp even though the heat emanating from the bulb felt good. His rest was undisturbed, and he awakened early as usual. The house was empty.

He opened the bread box to learn that there was no bread. Undeterred, he moved to the fridge and saw a can of Spam. He grabbed a fork and quickly finished the canned meat. After eating, Darin started picking up trash. Donna would party hard, and it would be up to Darin to clean the house even if he was not a part of the drinking.

Darin would drain any beer bottle that was not empty, or he would find a cap for any liquor and store it. He placed the empty cans and bottles in the bins that Donna created for recycling. Then he would wipe down the tables, vacuum, and mop. Under no circum-

stances was Darin to enter Donna's bedroom or bathroom. He didn't
know why, but he feared her and therefore obeyed.

As he was finishing cleaning, he heard Donna's van pull up.
Quickly, he rushed to his room and got into bed. He heard two sets
of footfalls and knew that Donna was not alone. Darin exhaled and
continued to wait. He listened as the two entered her bedroom, but
the sound stopped. After a few moments, there was laughter, and the
tempo of the footsteps seemed lighter. They left, and the door shut.

Darin wondered what they came to get, and he wrestled with
the urge to go into her bedroom. Curiosity got the better of him on
this day, and he went into her room. Now that the threshold was
crossed, there was no restraining his actions. He opened the nightstand drawer and saw glass pipes, needles, and a spoon. Continuing
his search, in the closet he found a plain box on top of spare blankets.

With deftness, he opened the box, and inside was cash. Donna was not broke; she had hundreds of dollars rolled up. He took the
rubber band off one roll and counted $1,000. There were four other
rolls. He assumed that Donna had five thousand dollars in cash in this
box. He rerolled the wad and rebanded it. Then he shut the box and
placed it back precisely where he had found it.

Donna did have money, but Darin had no plans for justice
or a confrontation. He searched out of unknown curiosity without
motive or intention. This was the first time he had defied his aunt's
command. With this new knowledge, he felt satisfied, like he felt when
buying his own pie. Never was he satiated, or even comforted.

Later that day, Donna returned looking tired; her eyes were
hollow, and she looked weak.

"Do you want the rest of my Chinese food, Darin?" Donna

asked as she placed the plastic bag with a red dragon picture on the counter.

"Yes," Darin said as he stood and moved towards her.

"Here, eat this one," Donna said as she placed the other boxes in the fridge.

Darin grabbed the box and was pleased the chopsticks were not thrown away. He was not very good at using them, but he liked to try.

"I am going to bed. I'll see you in the morning before Marty takes you to work. You have an appointment with your therapist tomorrow, and I want to talk to you before Marty takes you there."

With that, Donna shuffled to her room and shut the door quietly. Darin ate the food with relish and used the chopsticks like a shovel. After he was finished, he threw away the carton and went to his room. He hung up his clothes and got into his pallet after turning off the lamp and lay there in darkness.

"I do not like therapists," he muttered to himself.

"Tell me more . . ."

"Unpack that . . ."

"How do you feel?"

In the morning, Darin waited for his aunt to wake up. He sat motionless on the edge of the sticky couch in front of a large window. Darin turned on no lights; only the foggy morning light lit the room. Marty was rarely on time, and Donna would wake before Darin had to leave. She emerged from her room wearing a pink robe with stitched flowers, lit a cigarette, and sat near Darin. After a few drags, she rotated towards Darin and smiled.

"When you see your therapist today, tell her that your medication is not working anymore." Darin sat silently for a moment and then asked why she said that.

"No, Darin, it is not working. You need them to make it stronger or get a different medicine like Thorazine," Donna explained. "Don't worry; you just need to tell her that you have been having bad thoughts and that you think it might be the medication."

"I don't want her to send me away again," Darin whispered.

"She won't. Just tell her everything is okay, but you want to make sure."

"Okay, I will."

Donna put out her cigarette while lighting another. She then flung her head side to side, fluffing her hair.

"Do you ever talk about me?" Donna asked.

"No," said Darin.

"Good, they might send you away again if you talk about me," Donna informed him.

Donna got up and started boiling water to make coffee. Darin looked at her figure, which was highlighted by the tied rope, and felt ownership and then disgust. Marty's horn honked then, and Darin stood up and moved towards the door. He paused, dimly aware that more should be said, but Donna continued her efforts at the kitchen sink. Darin raised his hood and exited the home.

Chapter 4

Marty had dropped off Darin early for his appointment with his counselor. He had said he couldn't take Darin in the middle of the day because he had more to do, so Darin was early and sitting in the waiting room. The walls were covered in African masks and paintings of shapes with bright colors. On a table was an electric kettle with an assortment of herbal teas and several magazines for women. Darin felt uncomfortable in this waiting room that both insulted and repelled him.

Being forced by idleness, Darin picked up an issue of Psychology Today. He randomly flipped through the pages, reading the titles "Masculine Inheritance: Boys are not being raised to love," and "It is okay not to be okay: How to forgive the unforgivable," and "If God were Us, what would he say?" and "Return to the center: How to connect with the inner feminine." There he sat, reading psychological insights but learning nothing.

An hour or two passed, and Jessica opened the door as her client entered the waiting room. Both were teared up, and Jessica looked at the client with compassion, expressed by a tilted head and posture of motherly sympathy. As the client motioned to exit, Jessica extended her arms and offered one last hug. The client accepted, and they embraced like survivors of a shared tragedy. Neither person had noticed Darin.

As soon as the sobbing woman left the room, Jessica became erect and rigid.

"Hello, Darin," she said.

He looked up and locked eyes with his counselor. They held a gaze for a brief but tense moment, and then Darin said, "Hello."

"Would you like to come into my office?" Jessica asked with a practiced smile of warmth. Darin got up and moved towards the other room. She allowed him to enter first. When he had sat down, she asked if he would like any tea be he refused it. After a few moments, Jessica returned holding a greenish tea with both hands as she sat in her chair.

The office was decorated with pictures of Jessica and her friends, two degrees, and an assortment of books written by women for women. She wore strange clothes, but she was attractive. She was like a beautiful berry that seems edible but is never eaten out of instinct. Whenever Darin came to these sessions, he became uncomfortable. His hands seemed dirtier; his nails longer; and his clothes suddenly appeared ragged and slightly putrid. Darin only felt ashamed of himself compared to this woman and her curated space.

Jessica absorbed the heat from her teacup with both hands like a kitten suffocating a baby's breath. After taking two sips of hot tea, she sat the cup on a coaster, adjusted her glasses, and assumed a posture of presence. Without shame, the mental health expert pulled out her notes from their last session. Darin watched this process with irritation and growing malice. Finally, she looked up, feigned a smile, and asked with soft eyes how he was doing today.

"I am doing okay," he said, looking through her. She slowly readjusted herself in the chair and asked Darin how work was going next.

"I got in trouble Friday at work," he replied.

"Tell me more about that," she quickly launched.

"There was a woman there, and I was looking at her. She got mad, and so did Marty."

"Why did they get mad?" she inquired.

"Marty said that I was staring."

"Did you stare at her?" she said with sudden concern.

"I don't know," Darin blurted. His blood started to surge, and his hands got clammy. He became acutely aware of his breath and body. He wanted to lunge out of his chair, attack or retreat.

"Let's unpack that, Darin. Do you remember how you became my client?"

Darin nodded his head like a boy caught in a white lie. He remembered the incident that brought him to Jessica. After his mother died, Darin played on a slide in the park. A girl appeared and began teasing Darin for being slow he remebered.

"Watch out," the little girl said as she pushed past him at the top of the tall slide. Then she laughed and squealed with delight as she sped down the apparatus. Darin got to the top and awkwardly seated himself. The little gremlin then rushed up the steps again and began pushing Darin to go down the slide. He was scared to let himself down, and she started forcing him.

"Do it, do it!" the girl exclaimed with tyranny. Darin gripped the handles with terror as she began to push harder.

"Stop!" said Darin.

Laughing, the child pushed and prodded him until his grip released, and Darin violently descended. He landed on his back and felt pain and rage. Instinctively, he picked up a large rock and threw it at the girl. Immediately, it hit her head, and she tumbled over the edge. Darin thought he had killed her, but in a few moments, she began to wail for her dad. Darin fled toward his aunt's house with the girl's father in pursuit.

"I almost killed a little girl at the park with a rock," Darin told Jessica. "Umm hmm, that's right. You have had a problem with women for a long time Darin.

Your behavior can make women not feel safe, and that is not ok," Jessica stated flatly.

"I was just looking at her watering her plants,"

"A look can mean many things to different people. Have you ever considered that?"

He sat silent momentarily and repeated that he was "Just looking."

"What did you feel when looking at her?"

"I thought she was pretty," Darin confessed.

"Unwanted sexual attention is assault, and women shouldn't be subject to unsolicited stares," the therapist lectured.

"I thought she was beautiful," Darin whispered, and lowered his head.

"What happened after?" Jessica inquired.

"The woman complained to Marty, and I almost got fired."

"You see? Inappropriate behavior hurts everyone, Darin."

Satisfied with herself, the expert allowed the topic to end. Silence followed, and she returned to her tea. Darin wanted out this room, out of his dirty clothes. Something profound in his core ground and milled. He saw himself through Jessica's eyes and hated her for it. Darin felt betrayed by Melissa. They had a moment, and there was an exchange between them.

"How are things at home?"

"They are good," Darin answered.

"How is your aunt?"

"She is okay."

"Is she working?"

"Yes, she is setting up for a big sale."

"A garage sale?" asked Jessica with some confusion. "I asked if she was working."

"She is," Darin repeated.

"What happened to her job at the groomer's?"

"She said that job was hurting her wrists, and she couldn't do it anymore," Darin answered.

(In reality Donna got caught stealing and was fired. Her addiction had started to get worse, and she needed money to fund it.)

"I see," said Jessica. "Are you helping with the expenses at home?"

"Yes, Marty gives Donna my money from work,"

"It is good to contribute, isn't it?" replied Jessica.

More silence followed, and Jessica quickly looked at her clock on the wall behind him.

"I don't have much time today, Darin, because my sister is in town, and we have a planned trip. Would you be okay with cutting our session short today?"

"I'm okay, but I have been having some thoughts I haven't had for a while," Darin blurted with embarrassment. "I think my medication isn't working right . . ."

"That's not a big deal, Darin. I can increase your dosage, and you can tell me if it helps in our next session."

Relieved by the session's early closure, Jessica emitted another summoned smile and stood. Her long necklace swayed by the weight of the lapis lazuli stone dangling between her breasts. With her arm, the counselor gestured for Darin to exit, and he did. As he left her office, he pierced a waiting client with his gaze. It was a woman, well-dressed and bursting with joy at the emergence of her therapist. As Darin moved across the room, the woman broke his stare and stood to embrace Jessica.

Before opening the door to exit the building, Darin noticed Donna was there to pick him up. Usually, he had to walk home after a session. With some reluctance, Darin moved to the passenger side of the station wagon. Donna leaned over to unlock the door, and Darin opened the door and began to enter the vehicle, but Donna told him to take off his hoodie because it was wet.

Darin got in with his garment in his lap. Donna looked at him with excitement.

"Did you tell her about the medication?" she asked.

"Yes," replied Darin.

"Well . . .?"

"She said that she can have the dosage increased."

"Good job, baby," Donna said before she started the car and backed out of the parking spot.

Darin sat motionless, observing the city through his window. The car wipers rhythmically pursued their purpose, and he leaned his head on the passenger window.

Chapter 5

Resentment burrows deep in our being, contorting and poisoning thoughts and beliefs. Marty and Darin were back at Melissa's property in Lake Oswego. Marty had told the owner that they would be back the next day, but he had started drinking again. Once Marty broke down and drank, he could not stop his ravenous thirst for liquor.

Donna had dropped Darin off at the work site after going to pick up his increased prescription for Chlorpromazine. She had given him one and kept the rest. She told him that it would be best if she held onto the medications because they were stronger now, and that it would be very important to not take too many or skip days. Darin was indifferent about who controlled the pills.

He got out of the car and watched her drive off. Donna was pleased and waved as she pulled away. Darin's body responded to his aunt's pleasant mood, and he felt a fleeting desire to go with her. He turned and saw Marty violently prepping the worksite. His vaporous feelings of goodwill vanished as he headed toward Marty and the truck.

"What the fuck took you so long?" Marty grumbled with perceivable hostility.

"I had to fill my prescription after my appointment," Darin flatly answered.

Darin made him uncomfortable, and that made Marty feel threatened, which aggravated his aggression towards Darin. With his peripheral vision, he noticed a pint of whisky on the truck seat. Today will not go well, he thought waiting for Marty to end his aggressive dominance.

"Get the post hole digger out and start digging holes where I've marked," he told Darin with lessened contempt.

Darin grabbed the tool and headed to the back of the house, where the new fence would be installed. The yard was mostly exposed mud and withered wood chips. The tranquility of the space had been destroyed by the loss of the old fence and the leveling of the earth. Disrupted yards caused wives of yuppies great distress. Small sanctuaries are of great value to the nesters of suburbia.

As Darin started to dig, he could feel eyes on him. He knew it was Melissa staring at him through the living room window. Darin kept his head down and smashed the implement with vigor. As he dug, he felt a deep inner restlessness. He didn't know where the angst came from, but a sudden feeling of the need to escape overcame him. Then he remembered that his medication had been increased, and the feeling remained. Still, remembering about his medication, he could now accept the urge rather than succumb to it's synthetic demand.

The ground was wet, and the air was damp, as was Darin. When the air was filled with moisture, thirst could go unnoticed. Darin's mouth was dry, but he resisted drinking water for two reasons. Marty would be furious if Darin abandoned his work—even for thirst. Secondly, the owner of the home continuously observed him. Darin knew she was lurking to find a reason to complain about his presence.

When Darin finished digging the new fence holes, he realized Marty had already placed the posts in the holes.

"Get up to the driveway and get the Quikrete offloaded," Marty commanded.

"Bring the bags here or cover them with a tarp in the driveway?" questioned Darin.

"What do you think?" Marty retorted with resentment.

Darin lumbered up the slope through the mud. His boots were covered, and he tracked footprints down the driveway where he would wait for the delivery driver. A few moments later, Al pulled up in a flatbed with several bags of Quikrete, along with some lumber and hardware. Al exited the truck, slowly flicked his cigarette into the gutter, and tightened his suspenders.

"What do you say, Darin?" Al questioned with bemusement.

"Putting in the posts for the fence," Darin flatly conveyed.

"Yep, I see that. Marty doing okay?"

"Yeah," Darin replied.

"Where do you want it," Al asked, accepting the rejection of small talk.

"I got to haul 'em to the back," answered Darin as he started undoing the straps.

"All right, I'll pull in the driveway and make it a little easier for ya."

Darin stopped undoing the tie-downs, and Al got back in the truck with some effort due to his girth. The vehicle started, and the belt squealed as Al maneuvered the flatbed and moved in reverse down the long driveway. Darin walked back to the front of the garage and waited for Al. The truck stopped in front of Darin, and he started unloading the cargo. Al remained in the truck smoking.

The Quikrete absorbed the moisture, and the escaping dust of the mixture made Darin's mouth even more dry as he humped the fifty-pound sacks down to the post holes. Darin finished staging the bags and began unloading the fence lumber. Marty was checking the holes' depth with his measuring tape. Darin knew that each hole was the exact depth that Marty had told him, but he still worried that one would be off.

"Is that Al?" asked Marty with slight sheepishness.

"Yeah," said Darin.

"Alright, start dumping these bags in the holes. I'll go talk to him."

Marty's face was pale, and he sweated without physical exertion. The anxiety of needing a drink was starting to show. Darin slashed open the first bag and slopped it into the post hole. Marty wiped his brow and headed up the slope to meet Al. The lights in the living room were on now because the sun had yet to perform its miracle.

As Marty approached, Al looked at him with a prolonged pause before rolling down the window.

"You owe me $175, bud," Al murmured with no animation.

"I know, Al. This lady will pay her first installment as soon as the posts are set." Marty confessed.

"You're always tight on cash, buddy; maybe you should lay off the sauce," said Al as he wrote in his ledger.

"I'm good for it, Al. Just give me a few days."

Without the slightest hint of humor, Al turned his face to

Marty's, "I want that money, and I want it soon."

Marty noticed a tire iron resting in Al's lap. He knew that Al would beat him to death if he didn't pay. Al had been floating drunks and convicts in the trades for many years, and his reputation needed little inflation to incite fear.

"We are setting the posts today, Al. I'll pay you as soon as I get the job finished," Marty stammered.

Al waved and returned to his notes. Marty quickly acknowledged the gesture and started unloading the lumber and the hardware. When Marty was done, Al slowly pulled out of the drive-way and was gone. Marty went to his truck and took a long pull of whiskey. It immediately warmed his face and gave him a moment's relief to his anguish. The paleness was gone, and fury took its place once again.

Just as Darin emptied the bags in the holes, Marty was on him to get the hose attached to the spigot. Darin was relieved that he would be able to get some water. Darin went to the work truck and saw there was no hose. Marty must have left it at another job. Darin returned empty-handed, and Marty exploded.

"I thought I told you to get the hose, boy," Marty shouted.

"There is no hose..."

"Oh, bullshit," said Marty as he marched up to the truck, slipping in the mud.

Darin followed, and Marty tore apart the tools, vainly searching for his hose. After intense rummaging, Marty realized it wasn't there, and his temper subsided.

"I'll just ask Melissa if she has one," Marty said, without acknowledging his abuse of Darin. He strutted to the front door and rang the bell. Instantaneously, Melissa answered.

"Ma'am, Darin forgot to bring our hose so we can mix the Quikrete. Do you happen to have one I can use?" Marty inquired.

"We have one in the garden shed, but I want it clean and re-hung when you're done."

"Absolutely!" Marty exclaimed with excitement and exaggerated gratitude.

"Also, I want those muddy footprints in my driveway sprayed off before you call it a day?"

"Of course, we never leave a job site a mess," Marty answered, concealing his malice for being pushed to defend his work ethic.

He stomped to the garden shed and found the hose hanging and coiled to perfection. Grabbing it, he headed to the spigot, connected the hose, turned it on, and went to the first hole. Darin licked his dry lips and waited to mix the concrete and water. They worked quickly, in a rhythm set by Marty's frustration.

After mixing the Quikrete with water, they began nailing support boards on the posts to keep them level and plumb. He could move quickly under pressure, and fear was the only thing that made him perform. Marty was usually lazy and inefficient with his labor. Today, he was pressed to execute his tasks by a mounting need to drink and by realizing the brutal consequences of debt to Al.

Marty went to collect a payment from Melissa as soon as they were done. Darin grabbed the hose and drank deeply. The water ran down his chest, giving him a chill, but he kept guzzling. After satisfying his thirst, he cleaned, coiled, and hung the hose in the garden shed. As soon as he had secured it, Marty returned and told Darin to clean the driveway.

"That bitch won't pay unless you clean up that mess you

made," Marty hissed. With a tremor, Darin reached back up, but he started shaking violently before grabbing the hose. He began rhythmically convulsing with eyes full of bewildered terror. Marty watched in shock as Darin lost control and fell backwards, hitting his head.

Chapter 6

Loss of conscience in the presence of brutes ensures that some form of molestation or injury will transpire. There was sunshine, tranquility, and content. Darin was in a yard with terraced garden beds housing sunflowers and lavender. The open areas were hedged by cherry blossoms and were in full bloom. A cool breeze and radiant heat mixed, bringing Darin profound peace.

The sky darkened, the wind came, and the trees shed their flowers. Pink blossoms swirled around Darin and touched his face. The dramatic change in the environment unsettled Darin. He resisted the profound shift and tried to summon back the serene experience, but the beauty was gone. Soon, the blossoms were whipping him with incessant violent force,

Marty startled Darin, delivering blow after blow. Manifestations of pleasure and terror glimmered across his visage. Darin held on to his dream with determined futility. Still, Marty's strikes tore away any chance of returning to his garden. With great malice, Marty struck Darin again, and his eyes opened. Reality returned, and Darin was mounted by a wet tyrant and was in physical distress.

"Is he alive?" Melissa whimpered. Marty answered Melissa while holding eye contact with Darin.

"I got him now," Marty responded, partially satisfied with his rescue and reluctant that the dramatic event was over.

Darin tried to grab Marty's throat with murderous speed, but his arms barely responded and rose slowly with limp wrists. Darin had no energy, no power, and his body could not react to its command. Pleased with himself, Marty recovered and stood straddling Darin as a conqueror.

Darin writhed in the dirt of the floorless garden shed. A power deep within him propelled him to rise. Melissa and Marty stood awestruck as Darin growled and grunted like a beast in its death throes. Finally, Darin got on all fours and felt his inner being regain connection with his animate body.

Darin gripped the mud with hatred. A full manifestation of murderous toxication seized his entity. As he began to rise, his legs failed him by weakness and tremor, and he remained on his knees and hands. The failure of his legs abated the coming violence that would have resulted in death. Darin's possession receded as a tide went out, and all that remained was confusion and anguish.

Melissa began to panic, and Marty tried to calm her.

"I want you off of my property this very instant," Melissa said with dilated pupils.

"He is alright; he just had an accident. That's all," Marty insisted, shamefully accepting Melissa's command.

The tone, demeanor, and command of Melissa's bearing communicated that there was little time to flee.

With a screeching wail, Melissa repeated herself. "Get out of here, now!"

Marty, realizing that Melissa would call the police, grabbed Darin and snatched him to his feet. "Get your ass in gear and move," Marty whispered. Darin knew something was wrong, but the timing of his mental and physical reaction was delayed. Marty slung one of Darin's arms around his shoulder and grabbed him around his waist. They began to slog up the incline. Marty could feel the density of Darin's frame as they gained ground. There was power within Darin that Marty instinctually feared.

As they neared the truck, the rain began to assault them. Marty stabilized Darin against the vehicle, opened the door, and motioned for Darin to enter. With more authority in his arms than legs, Darin pulled himself into the truck. Staring straight ahead, Marty shut the door with some trepidation. Marty hesitated a moment at the back of the work truck.

He wondered if he should try to calm Melissa and get paid for their labor again. He looked and listened, hoping to sense her whereabouts and emotional state. Then he saw her in the house through the window on the phone. She was manically pacing, and her features were hysterical. With resignation, Marty walked to the driver's side of his work truck, opened the door, started the engine, and drove away slowly.

As they exited the driveway, Marty sighed. His aggression and quickness were replaced with resignation and acceptance. "I'm going to take you home now, Darin," Marty said flatly without orienting himself to receive a response. "There will be no work tomorrow or any other day," Marty concluded.

As they drove, both men were silent. Marty was defeated

by chance, fate, and circumstance. He knew that he couldn't return to Melissa to get paid. He had no insurance as he was not a bonded craftsman. Al would be expecting payment, and he always got what he was owed.

Darin was locked in a trance. He heard Marty but did not react to the loss of his employment. He was mourning the loss of his dream and enduring the bewilderment of reality. They moved through the city like castaways resigned to their fate. Unlike his usual vehicle operation of reckless speed and decisiveness, Marty was controlled and drove lawfully.

Marty pulled into the driveway of Donna's house without putting the truck in park. Darin opened the door, exited, and walked towards the house. He left the door to the truck open, but Marty did not yell at him to shut it. He drove the vehicle, gave the gas pedal a quick thrust, and then sharply engaged the brake. The door closed, and Marty put the truck in reverse and left.

Surmounting the steps was difficult for Darin. His body felt drained. Each step took more energy than expected. The process of ascending with struggle only deepened Darin's resolve to remaster himself. He found the spare key under the moldy, barren plant pot. He unlocked the door, crossed the threshold of the living room with muddy boots, and descended to his lair.

Darin opened his eyes in the darkness. He lay motionless but alert. He could hear heavy footsteps pacing the floor above him. Donna was home, and Darin could discern that she was upset and panicked. He closed his eyes and became aware of his body. He was wet, thirsty, in pain, and hungry. It quickly drove him to his feet. He reached for the knob on the lamp and rotated it. The bare bulb illuminated his dwelling. He removed his boots and wet socks, headed to the bathroom, and paused in front of the mirror.

There, gazing at him, was a familiar yet foreign face. Darin paused briefly, aware that a reflection should not be alien. Disengaging from the acute jolt of unfamiliarity in his image, he turned on the water and drank deep drafts. Like a beast at a trough, Darin consumed; he took no pleasure in quenching dehydration. He only desisted when his thirst was abated.

Donna swiftly cascaded down the stairs. Darin had already made his way back to his pallet and curled up in a fetal position. Donna opened the door and stood at the threshold of the room. Her silhouette was exaggerated by the back lighting causing a magnification of her presence. Her shadow towered over Darin; her messy hair created a menacing outline permeated with evil.

"Why are you home," Donna questioned.

Without rolling over to face Donna, Darin stirred and shifted.

"I got sick at work, and Marty had to take me home," Darin explained.

"You tracked mud from the front door to your room," Donna continued.

With effort, Darin shifted and rolled to face Donna. Her face was hidden by darkness, but her demeanor was growing in malice.

"I want you to get up and clean this house before I beat the living shit out of you," Donna stated with cold clarity.

"I will, as soon as I feel normal," said Darin.

Donna entered the room with phantom-like calmness and began to beat Darin with an old leather razor strop. Darin lay motionless and absorbed the thrashing. Crying out would only incite Donna to rage. She would pause between blows, discerning whether her last lash impacted pain. If Darin twitched or whimpered, she would focus on that area and increase her force and precision.

"I want you to clean up this mess," Donna said with exhaustion.

"I will, as soon as I feel better," said Darin, staring into the location her eyes might be.

There was a moment of stillness. Donna lingered in her towering position. Unsure if more strikes would descend, Darin braced himself and held his breath. The phantom withdrew, and the cold darkness embraced Darin in his anguish. One of the strop hits had landed above Darin's eye, and blood was flowing down his face. He could smell the iron and feel the blood slowly oozing. Darin felt a sense of contentment from the laceration. The agony that he was enduring was materialized in a weeping wound.

This exquisite pain gave Darin peace, and he was able to breathe. The exhaustion and disorientation drained away. His body was no longer a foreign landscape of unfamiliar sensation. He stretched out of the curled position and breathed deeply. In this moment of alignment, he closed his eyes, smiled, and slept.

Darin became conscious, and a moment of panic overcame him as reality forced its way through the remnants of the depths. He was alive, not dreaming. The medication had worn off, and he felt adjusted and coherent. He reached for the gash above his eye and felt the flakes of crusted blood. Touching the wound centered Darin, and he felt comfort.

He sat up and got his boots. They were covered in dry mud, and he took them to the bathroom sink. He turned on the hot water and waited. The sensation of cold water running across his fingertips agitated him. Waiting for the water to warm locked him in the presence that he wanted to escape. With relief, Darin felt the water begin to warm. He placed a boot under the faucet and began to claw the clay mud off.

He placed his wet boots in the tub and went to his room to get dressed. Natural light pierced his cave through the glass block windows. He stood in the center of his room and gloried over his bruises and cuts. Each blow had left a mark, and Darin touched each mark. As the pale light illuminated his pallid body, he moved his hands with sensuality and tenderness. And when the ceremony was over, he found his damp clothes, dressed, and moved towards the stairs to the upper floor. The house was clean, and Donna was gone. He found a note on the kitchen counter. I cleaned up the mess. There is a sandwich in the fridge. - I cannot get ahold of Marty. Do you know where he is? Take your medicine.

Darin opened the refrigerator and removed the plate with the bologna sandwich. Next to the food was a pill, just like the one Darin had taken the day before.

He took the plate to the couch and ate the sandwich. Then he got up, filled a glass with water, and returned to the coach. He placed the glass next to the plate and stared at the pill. A moment of rebellion encompassed his thoughts; maybe he shouldn't take the prescription. The resistance was brief, and he took the pill, drank some water, and swallowed it.

Chapter 7

Darin cleaned the plate and glass, dried them, and put them away in their proper place. As he did, he remembered getting sent away to the institution after the death of his mother and the attempted murder of the little girl on the slide with a rock. Donna had called the police after Darin refused to clean the house. "If you do not do as I tell you, I'll get you sent away!"

"I don't know how to clean," Darin cried.

"I already showed you how little shit," Donna screamed. She shoved a dirty rag into his limp hands and grabbed them, forcing him to scrub. With great force and emotion, Donna raged.

"Like this, you see?" Donna wailed.

Darin continued to scream and cry, and Donna became frantic.

"I told you, and now you're going to see," Donna said with sudden composure. She picked up the phone and called the police. The father of the little girl that Darin had assaulted with the rock on the slide had filed the incident with the police. Enraged with the attack on his daughter, the father relayed the details of the encounter with inflated and exaggerated details. The policeman who logged the crime was new to the force and was determined to protect the innocent. Officer Caliban was short for an enforcer, but he compensated for that trait with aggression, forcefulness, and brutality.

Darin sat exhausted on the floor. He had begged Donna not to get him sent away. After she called the police, Darin grabbed the dirty rag and, with naive zeal, started to scrub and wipe every surface in hopes of reversing Donna's decision. In childlike desperation, Darin had no idea that it was too late to reverse the course of action now set in motion.

Once he finished cleaning, he sat on the floor. Donna had not changed her mind, and the police were still coming. He sat in deflated hope. The death of his mother and the imminent departure from this home collided within him. He stared at his hands, the rag, and his aunt. His little hands could not save him. The dirty rag only spread the grime he was attempting to clean up, and he accepted that his fate belonged to the whim of others.

It was dusk when Officer Caliban arrived. He rapped on the door with the butt of his issued Mag flashlight. Darin made eye contact with him through the glass of the main entrance. There was no pity or understanding in the policeman's stare. Darin instantly knew that he was going to be taken and that he was now alone. Donna got up, walked to the door, and put on her countenance of civility. Her remarkable ability to shift personas was startling.

Officer Caliban entered the house without further invitation as soon as Donna cracked the threshold. The fabric of his uniform started to dry, and steam formed from the heat in the room.

"Is this the boy?" Caliban inquired to Donna.

"Yes, this is him. He was my sister's son, and I have been left with him," Donna answered. "Darin just told me about the girl that he hurt in the park, and I think he needs help and needs to take responsibility," Donna continued.

"Come here, son." Officer Caliban commanded.

Darin stood still, clutching the rag as if the connection to his labor might garner appreciation or even respect. Darin walked towards the imposing man with great anxiety and reluctance. An impending doom seemed to project itself from the policeman towards him. Darin flashed a glance at Donna as he approached Officer Caliban. Donna would not meet his gaze. She had cast him to the wolves, and there was going to be no intervention to recall the decision.

Darin stood a few feet away from the policeman with his head hung low and waited for the lawman's instructions.

"I said come here," uttered Officer Caliban, pointing his hand directly in front of him. Darin complied and stepped within little Napoleon's space.

"Now look at me," the young officer commanded.

Darin looked up and into the eyes of the policeman with fear, shame, and helplessness.

"Did you try to kill a little girl at the park with a rock a few days ago?"

Darin paused for a moment and then thought if he just agreed with Donna and the police officer, they may let him be. "Yes," Darin answered with no visible regret or defense.

Officer Caliban was a bit shocked at the immediate confession. Sudden surrender disjointed his preparation to interrogate, push, prod, and cajole. Darin thought for a moment that he was going to receive approval and leniency for his direct and immediate compliance. After regaining his posture of control and authority, Caliban grabbed the boy by the shoulders and leaned his head down to engage the child fully with the terror of authority. "You are going to be coming with me," the policeman announced with malicious enjoyment.

In a sudden flash of despair, Darin twisted his torso with great effort and tried to flee towards the stairs to his room. Officer Caliban was taken aback by the sudden resistance and lost his grasp on Darin's shoulders. Darin screamed and began to moan and wail frantically. In the tussle, Darin had accidentally struck the officer with his little hand. The impact of the blow gave permission to Officer Caliban to release his self-restraint like a brute to dominate the child.

The officer grabbed the boy by the neck, slammed him down on the ground, and wrenched his arms behind his back. He then straddled the child with unneeded violence and dominance. Donna screamed, but the outburst was not out of concern for Darin, but, rather, it was an instinctual response to sudden and aggressive movement. The officer handcuffed the boy tightly, being unaccustomed to the appropriate restraint needed for a child.

Once Darin was restrained and the officer had gained composure, the officer looked at Donna. "I am going to need you to come down to the station and fill out a report," he commanded.

Donna nodded her head with shock. She had not expected that she would have to file paperwork or go to the police station. She grabbed her coat and purse, first confirming that she had enough cigarettes. Officer Caliban stood Darin up, turned the boy around and glared at him. "You just struck an officer; that was a big mistake," Caliban informed Darin with barely controlled passion.

Darin only continued to sob, and he was manhandled out of the house. Down the stairs they trundled with jolts. Officer Caliban controlled Darin by twisting the handcuffs to inflict pain and compliance. As soon as Darin would take the direction, the officer would pivot the tension to redirect the movement. In this way they made their path to the patrol vehicle.

Officer Caliban opened the back door and shoved the boy into the car. He slammed the door and Darin sat up and looked through his tears and bewilderment out the rain-streaked window as his aunt and the officer talked. Darin could not hear them, but it was clear that they agreed. The exchange was brief, and Donna made her way to her sky-blue van. Officer Caliban opened the driver's door of his cruiser, removed his nightstick, and sat himself behind the wheel.

The policeman got on his radio and updated the station on the detainment of Darin. The dispatcher's response was cold and technical. It was a woman's voice on the other end. Darin had a glimmer of hope that she might intervene and offer sympathy or question Officer Caliban's reasoning for his actions. As Officer Caliban was finishing his report, he looked in the rearview mirror and met Darin's eyes.

Darin knew that he was alone and at the mercy of brutish strangers with no love or understanding. The tears dried on his face, and a part of him died. The part of the boy that could be nurtured, trained, and developed gave up and retreated. Good faith, trust, and hope evaporated within the possession of state authority. Darin had been surrendered by a family member that was meant to love, protect, and guide him. The boy died, starved of affection, and the man who was born would move through this world needing nothing from anyone.

The back seat of the cruiser was cold, hard, and smelled of bleach. The handcuffs cut into his wrists, causing intense pain. At first the agony of thin metal edges crushing and cutting his little wrists almost compelled him to beg the officer to loosen them.

As they drove, the intense sensation deepened and summoned in Darin the energy of defiance. He would ask for nothing; he would endure. Darin drew closer to the pain allowing it to signal to him the true state of his existence. After all, what was physical duress? Just a sensation; just a signal that can be interpreted in any way he chose. Instead of reacting, why not feel the cutting deeply and let it shape him.

The cop car was made well and drove with relative silence and smoothness. Darin had never been in a vehicle that hummed and responded without jerks, grinds, and delays. The swift, efficient transport of the cruiser seemed to insult his plight. The outer world was calm and not concerned or shaped by his inner turmoil. Hate took root in Darin in the back of that vehicle. The world around him was indifferent to his feelings. The slight hum of the engine, the muffled rain coating the car, and the callousness of Officer Caliban created a temporal space within Darin.

That space was filled with reimagined pain, acceptance of being at odds with authority, and reliance on an inner sanctum where sensations and external input would be transmuted, blunted, or rejected. Darin built within himself a fortress of refuge. The walls were thick; the door was barred; and the guards would never sleep again.

He and the officer arrived...Darin did not know where exactly. Officer Caliban shut off the car engine, exited, and opened Darin's door.

"Get out." the officer ordered.

Darin did as he was instructed. He had mastered the pain, but it returned when he moved. The officer was agitated by Darin's struggle to worm his way out of the car. Caliban grabbed the back of his shirt and dragged him out of the vehicle and stood him on his feet.

Darin could sense that the policeman's intensity had waned, and for that he relaxed a little as they made their way to the station. Darin had never been to a police station, and the little boy in him was excited for a moment. As they moved the tight cuffs cut more, and he lost his youthful curiosity and returned to vague bitterness.

The entrance was extremely illuminated. The moment they crossed the threshold, Darin's eyes had to squint. The floor made his shoes squeak, and florescent lights revealed his grim demeanor. He felt ashamed; the other people in the building had clean-cut hair, trimmed nails, and ironed uniforms. The building smelled of industrial cleanliness, and the bright lights left no shadows for retreat. He had entered another world, a reality shaped by order, law, and rigidness. Immediately he despised this place and the entities that operated the system of law enforcement.

No one looked at him as they hurried through the building. They were all occupied with their tasks. A dwindling part of him searched the eyes of the other officers to see if someone kinder would intervene and save him from officer Caliban. It would not be so; he was in the system now. Attention was given at predetermined times for bureaucratic needs.

When they arrived at Officer Caliban's desk, Darin was seated. Officer Caliban unlocked one cuff and relocked it to the chair where Darin was placed. Caliban left without giving instructions to Darin.

The urge to urinate dominated Darin after Caliban left. He sat and tried to get the attention of the other officers.

"I have to pee," Darin said.

An officer at another desk looked up and peered through his reading glasses.

"You have to hold it till officer Caliban gets back" he responded with indifference.

"I can't hold it," Darin said.

The officer that had first responded now ignored him. He just sat there reading. Darin did not continue his effort to get help from the other officers. He tried to squirm; he tried to ignore the need to relieve himself.

After what felt like ages Darin's body began to release the urine against his will. There was nothing he could do about it. His jeans began to darken as the relieving sensation of warm piss cemented his shame. Officer Caliban returned and immediately noticed the smell of urine and the wet spot on the floor.

"Why didn't you say you had to go to the bathroom?" Officer Caliban questioned with irritation.

"I did," said Darin.

Officer Caliban looked at the portly officer with the readers on. The heavy-set officer looked up again and with a slight look of self-amusement flatly answered. "I told him to wait a minute for you to return. I have to finish my report".

Officer Caliban internalized his anger at the other officer and aimed it at the little boy. "Next time you got to use the latrine, you better say so."

"I will," said Darin.

Officer Caliban left and returned with a janitor. He pointed at the puddle, and the man in the blue jumpsuit gave a look of contempt to Darin and mopped the urine and left.

Officer Caliban, uncuffed Darin, led him across the office to a row of chairs further from his desk, and re-cuffed him.

"Sit here and wait. If you have to use the bathroom, you need to tell me."

The other officers snickered slightly, revealing their true nature despite their professional costumes. Officer Caliban ignored their amusement and returned to his desk.

Darin sat on his chair with his legs dangling. His wet pants became uncomfortable, and the odor of urine, mixed with the dampness, highlighted his internal spotlight of shame. He was at the front of the office. He could not hide or make himself invisible. No one seemed to care or notice him, but Darin felt exposed, like a prop. There he sat enduring filth, urine, and abandonment, waiting for this time to pass.

Chapter 8

Darin was awakened by a woman. When he looked at her, he saw eyes that tried to be kind, but they were not genuine. She had a dixie cup and a honey bun.

"Are you hungry or thirsty?" the woman inquired.

"Yes, I am," said Darin.

The woman opened the honey bun, folded the wrapper halfway and handed it to Darin. He was ravenous and immediately devoured the bun. He had a dim awareness that the bun was wonderful, but he could not slow down to savor the treat. In an instant the dessert was consumed, and the woman handed the cup of water to Darin. He drank it and then looked at the woman.

"My name is Samantha, and I work with the Juvenile Justice System."

Darin waited for her to say more.

"I am going to take you to another facility, one for kids. I just need to ask you a few questions, and then we can go somewhere nicer. Sound good?" Samantha asked. Darin nodded while licking the remnant of frosting on the corners of his mouth.

Darin was questioned about the girl he had hit with the rock. He believed what he had been told and regurgitated it to Samantha. Darin told her that he had tried to kill her for pushing him down the slide. He found a rock and intentionally hit her in the head, hoping that she would die. Darin hoped that his cooperation would expedite his release. Confession was always faster than inquisition, but in the hands of state employees, the results were often the same.

Samantha then asked about Donna. "How does your aunt treat you?"

"Good. She gives me a place to live and food to eat," Darin responded.

"Does she play with you and be nice to you?" Samantha pushed further.

"Donna has a lot of work to do, and she doesn't have time to play," Darin answered.

"Has she ever hit you or touched you in an inappropriate way?" Samantha pressed.

Darin thought for a moment, remembering the attacks and punishments Donna had doled out. He was about to answer that she had beaten him and touched him. Then he realized that if he told on her, he would not be able to go home.

"No, never," Darin said. The rest of the questions were informational, and Darin had a hard time answering them. Where was he born? When did his mother die? Where was his father?

Darin was getting more upset because he could not recall facts about his mother and father. It did not mean that he didn't love them; he just didn't know. After what seemed like ages, the questions were over, and Darin was removed from the handcuffs and given over to Samantha's custody. As they entered the building, Darin looked at Officer Caliban.

They met eyes and Darin held his gaze. The officer became uneasy and broke eye contact. The boy realized that his small size made grown men uncomfortable, and this gave Darin a feeling of power for a moment. Then he focused on following Samantha, and they left the station. The sun was up, and the air was warm. Darin hoped that he would be taken home. "Where are we going?" he asked.

"First, we are going to a juvenile facility, but in time I think we will be able to find you a family to live with," Samantha answered. Darin realized that he had to go forward at the direction of these servants of authority.

Upon entering the building, Darin could sense an undercurrent of unarticulated suffering. There were no cries or play, just slight shuffling and controlled youthful energy. He was being placed in a holding facility for children. There were beds, incomplete plastic toy sets, and books with crayon marks on every page. Children kept their heads down, and guards loomed at every corner.

"You will stay here, and I will return when the State decides what to do with your case," Samantha told Darin.

"This is Officer Gutiérrez, and he will take care of you," Samantha said as she looked to the officer to introduce himself. Officer Gutiérrez looked down at Darin and, with a glint of pleasure, put his hand on Darin's back and spoke. "Don't worry, little brother. We will get you sorted."

Darin cringed at the man's touch; it was soft but not kind. His body revolted at the contact, visibly offending the officer. "Go on and get yourself situated at that cot," Gutiérrez directed.

Darin began moving but paused to look to Samantha for confirmation. She did not acknowledge Darin's silent plea; her attention was on the other officer. They exchanged words, and she left. Upon her exit Darin felt a cold shiver. Officer Gutiérrez's gaze followed him and penetrated his internal integrity.

Darin made his way to the cot that had been pointed out to him by Gutiérrez. The other children watched him. They did not stare, but they paid attention. Exhausted from sleeping on hard chairs, Darin lay down and tried to close his eyes. The lights were too bright to sleep in this institution outside of regular hours. It was a feat only for the truly exhausted or the medicated.

The moment he drifted off, Officer Gutiérrez approached him and ordered Darin to follow him. Slowly he got up and stood. The officer had an aura of urgency that Darin was trying to meet, but grogginess and disorientation delayed his rousing. Gutiérrez grabbed him by the back of the shirt and lifted Darin to his feet. "Ándale, ándale," Gutiérrez insisted as he led Darin away from the open bay. Darin responded with compliance once his body was animated. The grip of the officer loosened as Darin started to move by himself. They entered a room with showers and sinks; not a bathroom but a station.

"You need to get clean, chico. You smell like piss," the officer lisped.

Darin paused; he did not want to undress and shower in front of this man. "Here?" Darin inquired.

"Where do you think? Yes, here," Officer Gutiérrez insisted.

Darin lowered his head and started to undress. All that he could see was the boots of the guard as he hesitantly surrendered to the command. One boot tapped rapidly with impatience and anticipation. Something switched in Darin, and he raised his head, locked eyes with the onlooker, and emanated defiance.

"I'm not undressing in front of you, faggot," Darin bluntly uttered.

Unused to resistance, Officer Gutiérrez stammered in shock. He composed himself and moved closer. He leaned close to the boy's ear and whispered. "It's going to be a long stay for you, vato; you don't want to make it worse," Gutiérrez said reclaiming his authority.

Darin held Gutiérrez's stare as the guard straightened himself.

"I'm not doing it," Darin said, with stoic resolution.

Gutiérrez's eyes glazed with menace. He had never been flatly resisted by a child before. He began to grab Darin when another guard entered the room.

"What's going on in here," said the new guard with authority.

Gutiérrez whirled around and responded, "This kid pissed himself. He needs to get clean clothes and a shower."

"You know that there has to be two guards if a kid is going to shower without the rest of the group." the other officer stated flatly.

Looking at the boy the man said, "Go ahead, son, and get cleaned up."

Darin moved away and finished undressing with some privacy as the other officer engaged Gutiérrez by making him turn his back to Darin. The shower was freezing. There was no indicator for hot water. Darin tried to find a position that would warm the water, but he could not.

With a shout, but with avoided eyes, the tall guard said, "Use soap."

Darin did as the man instructed and used the soap, but it had hardly lathered before the officer said, "Get out, dry off, and put these on."

Darin looked over his shoulder and saw the folded clothes provided by the officer who had intervened.

The issued articles were ill fitting but clean. Darin was relieved to be clothed and unmolested.

"Get back to your cot," commanded the orderly officer.

Gutiérrez tried to steal a look from Darin, but the boy ignored the glare and moved deftly to his cot as instructed. Entering the bay, the other boys stared at Darin, searching for confirmation of their fears. Darin held his head up with his shoulders back. The other children seemed to be awestruck by Darin. Nothing was said, but Darin had escaped Gutiérrez, and it was obvious to the other victims.

"Lights out in five minutes," boomed a voice that filled the bay. All the boys rushed to their cots and lay down. Darin did the same with calm efficacy.

The bright lights went off one row at a time, traversing the open area with methodical doom. The darkness of the cell bay was outlined by dim lights illuminating the guards as they stood sentry over the little outcasts. Silence allowed real sound to rise, and boots squeaked; keys jingled; and children sobbed in pillows. Darin could hear his own breath. Then he heard the subdued agonies that only night could reveal.

Darin began to drift asleep when Gutiérrez made his rounds and paused at the boy.

"I am not done with you, chica," said Officer Gutiérrez.

Darin didn't look at him but could feel the resentful wrath.

"Que duerma bien la pequeña," whispered Gutiérrez.

Dain didn't know what the guard said, but he knew it was a threat. In that moment, Darin vowed to himself to die rather than be touched by this man.

Darin's mouth was covered, and he was being pulled from his cot. Large eyes bulged around him staring on in frozen shock. The sweaty man grabbed and controlled him with deftness. A profound urgency took hold of Darin, and he struggled in the grips of the predator. Like a serpent, the guard began to control him. With his free hand Darin shoved his thumb into the eye of a portly assailant.

Darin could feel his digit penetrate that socket. Gutiérrez involuntarily cried out in sharp pain. He released the boy and quickly slithered away. Darin's heart was pounding, and he could hardly breathe. The attacker was gone as quickly as he had struck. Darin was damp with fear, and for the rest of the night he stood vigil over himself.

He met the daylight unrested, unsure, and alone. The other children avoided him. Instinctually the boys distanced themselves from the target of the hunter. Proximity to weakness was resisted by anyone wishing to survive in captivity. Darin subconsciously understood the position of the other boys and made no effort to gain allies.

Donna had filed her report with Officer Caliban, and Darin was now in custody. She was pleased with herself. Darin was of no use to her, and she resented sharing her home and food with him. Ever since her sister died, Darin had been a burden to her. Her sister's death was now complete in her eyes.

Donna was rummaging through boxes of treasure that she

would be selling soon. She had done well this week hitting all the yard sales early. She had a gift for haggling and perceiving quality. At one of the last yard sales, she had discovered a box of costume jewelry from the thirties. Only a few items had missing stones, and many of the pieces were marked by their makers. What drew her was a headdress made by Hobe.

She tried it on in the mirror and imagined that she was beautiful. Her masculine features were highlighted by the foreign adornment, but she pretended anyway. She knew some cabaret girls who would pay a good price for such a piece. She removed the headpiece and found a jewelry box that was large enough to store a festive crown.

As she returned to her loot, the phone rang. She ignored the intrusion and continued her inventory. The telephone rang again, and Donna could no longer block the repetitive alert. "Yeah," Donna blurted with unconcealed annoyance.

"Is this Donna Mallory?" asked the effeminate male voice.

"It is," Donna responded with a gruff, domineering tone.

"My name is Linus Doux. I'm a social worker for the state of Oregon."

"What is the problem now?" Donna said with exhaustive irritation.

"No problem, ma'am. I just wanted to make a last effort to find a suitable home for Darin," answered Linus.

"I thought he was already taken care of," Donna fired back.

"Well, he is being housed at a state facility for boys until there is a sentencing," Linus replied with the audible lament.

"So, what do you need from me then?" retorted Donna with a tone of finality.

"I wonder, Miss Mallory, if you knew that the State could incentivize a relative to be a caretaker for a child? We like to keep families together, and we understand that an unexpected dependent can be an financial burden you hadn't planned on," Linus explained.

Almost without thought Donna began to dismiss what Linus had informed her. However, the opportunity for more income restrained her impulsivity. "How much does the State pay?" Donna asked.

"The stipend differs based on the needs of the child and the caretaker, but the flat amount is $150 a month per child," Linus informed Donna.

When Donna got off the phone with the social worker, she felt pleased. She would be responsible for Darin if it meant that she would be compensated. She was able to take custody of Darin. She would be required to enroll him in a psychological assessment program, and he would be on juvenile probation for the assault on the little girl.

Within a few days Donna appeared to pick up Darin from the boys holding facility. Girded with authority and the promise of compensation, Donna's outward concern for Darin's swift return home expedited the transfer process. Officer Gutiérrez approached Darin on his cot.

"Your nodriza has come," Gutiérrez said with a strange mix of regret and resentment.

Darin was not sure what the officer meant, but he did understand that Gutiérrez wanted him to follow. Darin got up and followed the officer with trepidation. Gutiérrez had found another boy to haunt due to Darin's resistance, but Darin did not feel confident that Gutiérrez had given up on finding a way to rape him.

As Darin followed the monster, he could sense the pent-up rage the man harnessed by daylight because of the presence of other officers. Darin wondered how it was that such men remain hidden in plain sight. As they walked, Gutiérrez took on an aura of forced sincerity. "I just try to scare the chicos. You understand?" Gutiérrez stammered.

Darin nodded.

"It is best if you stay silent because I will deny it, and you will be held here longer," the officer suggested with common sense.

Gutiérrez stopped and looked at Darin. The boy glanced up at him and asked, "Where are we going?"

"As I told you, your aunt is here to take you back," Gutiérrez said in perfect English.

"I understand," said Darin.

Pausing to divine Darin's face, the officer smiled with content and continued moving.

"You're lucky, niño lindo," Gutiérrez expressed with a mix of compassion and regret.

Darin followed. He would not speak to anyone about Gutiérrez. There would be no point. Who would believe him, and it could cause him to linger in custody longer. Darin was relieved to be free of the Spanish spider and cared little for the other boys' fate.

As they reached the end of the bay, Darin saw Donna through the reinforced glass. Her eyes were wet with tears, and Darin felt a sensation of hate for her. Gutiérrez paused at the door, looked around to make sure no other boys were in the facility, and nodded to the guard on the other side. The sound of the unlocking door was mixed with authority and precision. In that instant, Darin felt more like himself, like a part of him was returning from a long journey.

After a few formalities, Darin and Donna walked out of the facility and made their way to Donna's van. The sun was blinding, and Darin felt sensations that he had ignored inside. All at once he felt bloated, confused, and sluggish. The light of day and the promise of home released him from a state of rigid emotional siege, and he began to cry. Donna opened the door and told him to get in.

She sat in the driver's seat and lit a cigarette. Annoyed by his outburst, Donna took a long drag and audibly exhaled. Darin was trying to swallow his emotions, but that only produced an outpouring of overwhelming sensations. Donna waited, and Darin could sense that she was growing impatient. He found a spot within himself and clung on like a castaway to a life buoy.

"Things are going to be different now, Darin," Donna started. She took a long pull from her unflicked cigarette. "I am legally responsible for you now. You have to do what I say when I say it," Donna finished.

With great effort to hold himself together, Darin responded with "Okay."

Donna put on her oversized sunglasses, became conscious of her extended ash, and tapped it in the ashtray. She paused for a moment but decided she was satisfied for now and started the van. With one turn of the key, the van cranked; with the second turn of the key, the van started.

Chapter 9

Darin snapped back to the present. Donna wanted to know where Marty was. She had cleaned up Darin's mess, made him food, and set aside his medication. Darin knew that he should immediately find out what happened and where he was or she would be after him too. He assumed that Marty was somewhere drunk, but there was a possibility that Al had gotten ahold of him too.

Darin put on his wet-but-mudless boots, grabbed his framing hammer, and left the house. Behind Donna's house was a section of undeveloped land. Blackberry bushes controlled the route and forced Darin to navigate rather than cut across the wild acreage. This was the fastest way to Marty's house, but Darin had stopped taking this path when one of Marty's neighbors got a large brindle bullmastiff.

The last time Donna sent Darin to Marty's to get paid for a week, Darin had experienced a violent encounter with the beast. Darin had hopped the fence and rounded the corner of Marty's neighbor's trailer, and the sentry was there. Without barking, the bullmastiff lunged at Darin with lethality. Darin retreated, but the feral animal pursued.

With only moments to spare, Darin jumped over the fence face first as the dog bit his leg.

There Darin sat face-to-face with the bullmastiff. His leg was bleeding, and his pants were ripped. The large dog began to bark, but it was not to alert his owners to an intruder. Instead, it was an expression of frustration that Darin had escaped him. Darin sat there and looked at the powerful animal with reverence and revenge. Two entities locked eyes, and the unkept beast stopped barking and stared.

Jack, a Hells Angel, exited the trailer with alarm, a revolver in his hand. He came up to the dog and gripped his pronged choker collar. The dog sat without breaking eye contact with Darin. "What the fuck are you doing?" asked the tall man with wild gray hair.

"I was coming to see Marty," responded Darin as he stood.

Best you don't cut across my property again," said Jack as he slipped the nickel-plated .357 behind his belt that was buckled by a confederate flag. Darin nodded and started walking away. The biker stood still and watched Darin sulk away for a moment as if to assert dominion.

Darin came to the fence again as he had the last time the bullmastiff attacked him. He pulled out his 23 oz. framing hammer, removed his hoody, and wrapped the wet garment around his arm. Then he observed for a moment, surmounted the fence, and dropped down silently. On the other side he paused, controlled his breath, and acknowledged the sensation of power in his body.

He stood and began to move forward with hunched legs and his wrapped arm forward with his hammer arm engaged. As expected, the bullmastiff appeared, contorted, and then attacked at a full sprint. Darin descended the hammer and made complete contact. The dog fell. Darin raised the hammer again with a spin and struck the canine with the claw side of the tool.

By instinct the dog continued to try to rouse an attack, but its body was unable to respond to the automatic impulse. Darin angled his arm to keep the dog pinned down. With the hammer claws embedded in the beast's head, little leverage was needed. Darin observed the mutt as its life drained. What had once been a source of fear was nothing more than a helpless puppy. The dog died, and Darin smiled.

Darin stood, removed the hammer from the dog's head with some effort, unwrapped his hoodie from his arm and put it back on. Then he wiped the blood of his hammer on the dog's body, stood and hid the hammer under his sweater. The Hells Angel's Harley was gone, to Darin's relief. There was no telling how long the biker would be away, so Darin quickly moved towards Marty's trailer.

Marty's truck was parked out front, and his door was open behind the closed screen door. Darin walked up the few steps and leaned against the tattered screen. The trailer smelled of old alcohol and laborers' remnants. Marty's place was riddled with rubbish.

"Marty . . . you home?" Darin called out in a deep voice.

Silence responded.

Darin was about to grab the handle of the screen door, but the dog's blood on his hand stopped him. He stood for a moment and then remembered that Al and Marty had had words earlier.

Darin turned from the screen door, found a water spigot, and washed the hammer and his hands as best as he could without soap. Darin liked how he felt. The dog was no longer a threat, and fear had been replaced by violence. Darin believed he felt how a man would feel. As he walked to Al's shop, a certain lightness of being overcame him, and he moved with less inhibition.

***

The bell rang as Darin walked into Al's hardware store. Darin paused and looked to see if he was going to be acknowledged. No one was at the counter, and the store was empty of customers. Al supplied most of the contractors that needed fronts because they had limited cash. Drunks, felons, and grifters could come to Al and get construction materials if they were willing to pay the interest fees.

The turbulent life of addicted tradesmen returned a handsome profit for the large and shrewd man. Al had a reputation for swift violence toward anyone who did not pay. Marty had complained that he was going to have to get a front by Al. Even in Marty's arrogance and self-aggrandizement, there was reality. Pay back Al or Al takes back.

Darin walked in and stood at the counter. There was a chrome call bell on the counter, but Darin did not ring it. A muffled sound emanated from the back, and a giant of a man slowly encroached with reluctant duty. Al's body moved with control and power despite his obesity. Al never rushed, but his approaching demeanor incited dread. Darin stood and maintained eye contact with the man.

"Yes?" Al said as he stopped at the counter.

"I'm looking for Marty," Darin said with flat directness.

"Hmm, aren't we all?" Al responded.

Darin paused.

"Marty has gone missing, and I know that he owes you money," Darin told Al without the trepidation the large man had become accustomed to.

"He does owe me money, and I will find him. But I have not

set eyes on the man since I dropped off the materials in Lake Oswego."

Darin had difficulty sensing lies, but he could detect an undercurrent of resentment. Al would not be bitter if he had extracted his pound of flesh as repayment.

"If you see him, will you tell him that Donna wants him to call her?" Darin requested.

"If I see him, you will know. And if I don't see him, I will be calling on Donna," Al uttered with his fleshy lips greedy to settle debt.

Darin held the gaze of the brute, securitized his eyes for truth, and accepted Al's words.

"Donna doesn't owe anything," Darin argued.

"Oh, but she does." Al retorted with subtle glee. "You're a good boy, and I have no problem with you. Go tell your aunt to come down here and pay me or find Marty and make him pay his debts," Al said with finality.

Darin felt the hammer under his hoodie and had an urge to smash the ogre's face like he had done with the bullmastiff. A rush of ecstasy coursed through his body. Who was this man that he wouldn't crumble as any other to the descending force of steel? Darin's leg began to quiver with an injection of adrenaline.

No stranger to the ways of men and violence, Al reached under the counter and pulled out an old Colt 911. Without pointing it at Darin, he flashed the weapon as a reminder of who was in charge. For a moment Darin thought he could take the fat bastard anyway; but reality returned, and Darin abandoned the idea.

"Like I said, you're a good boy, and I got no problem with you. I haven't seen Marty, but I want my money," Al expressed with complete control of emotion.

The fear of death didn't stop Darin, but the reality of the pistol and the obstacle of the counter compelled him to abate his rage. A tinge of regret neutralized his wrath, and he uncoiled. With the dissipation of imminent bloodshed, both men resumed a bearing of placidness.

"I will tell her what you said."

"Don't come back here unless the debt has been settled," Al said with cold authority.

Darin nodded almost imperceptively and turned to leave. Al stood sentry, projecting complete confidence. Darin headed for the front door as a shadow retreated from a growing light. The bell rang above him as he opened it, and Darin was back in the world.

Chapter 10

The rain had paused, and the clouds allowed the sun to shine. The glow warmed Darin's face, and for a moment everything felt right.

Colors were vivid, smiles of pedestrians were genuine, and roads led to places that were good. The sun vanished, and the glow was lost. The clouds usurped the light, and the shadows filled the void. Darin tightened his hood and made his way home like a deserter from a lost battle.

Marty most likely left town to avoid Al's retribution. There was also the possibility that Al had murdered him, or that he was simply drunk in a sordid place. Donna had instilled loyalty to the family that Darin had internalized. Darin did not like Marty, but he was committed to him. Marty was gone; Darin was unemployed; and Donna would be troubled.

Making his way home, Darin wrestled with two feelings unable to coexist in harmony. He was tired and longed for a refuge. He dreaded home but had nowhere else to go except the bridge. Donna would be expecting an update on Marty's whereabouts, and if he went to his underpass hideout, her anger would only intensify. Darin would return home to explain to Donna what Al had said and then escape to his spot if needed.

By the time he made it home, it was evening. The lights were on, and the sounds of guttural, debauched women in their cups were clear. Nights like these were strange and chaotic. Perhaps Donna and her friends would be happy to see him or would be instantly enraged at his return without knowing Marty's location. Darin looked through the window before entering. Donna and Shannon were sitting on the couch together smoking, drinking, and singing along to "Free Bird" by Lynyrd Skynyrd.

This pleased Darin because they appeared sentimental, and Skynyrd always pacified Donna. Darin entered, and the two women raised their beers in unison as they sung the lyrics. This made Darin blush, and the two women cackled with pleasure, pleased with their feminine power.

Donna got up and brought Darin a beer. He took it as he stood rigid despite Donna's intoxicated suppleness. She flung her arm around Darin and started dancing and continued singing while holding his eyes. Shannon laughed in the background, and that only encouraged Donna to press on with her uncomfortable hostage.

Realizing that Darin would remain uptight, Donna snickered and stumbled back to her couch. Darin remained standing, and the two harlots carried on without him. Donna waved him to come, and Darin responded by approaching and sitting next to Donna.

"Shots!" Shannon yelled as the song reached its climax. Donna grabbed the Jack Daniels and began liberally pouring three drinks into red party cups. Darin did not want to drink but refusing a shot was taboo. With the beer he could sip and pretend to partake. But shots were a direct demand to participate, and any refusal would cause conflict.

The whiskey burned, and a sensation of peace almost immediately engulfed Darin's whole sense of self. Warmness pulsed throughout his body, and Darin loved it. The women cheered after downing their drinks, and each lit another cigarette. Darin basked in his alcoholic glow and smiled.

The cassette tape concluded, and the spell of the music ended. Shannon sat back surrendering to her intoxication. Donna, who was never completely incapacitated by large volumes of spirits, turned towards him with hard eyes. Darin knew that she would not have forgotten about her request for him to find Marty.

"Did you find out where Marty is?" Donna snapped.

"No, I went to his house and to Al's shop," Darin said with an obedient countenance.

Shannon giggled, which irritated Donna.

"Something funny?" Donna slurred with instant authority.

"No, no . . ." Shannon responded, wishing to remain free of Donna's aggression.

Donna turned back to Darin and waited for more information, but Darin sat in silence. "What did that fat bastard say?" Donna asked with a lower tone while leaning towards Darin.

"He said that he hasn't seen Marty, but he wants his money," Darin replied.

"Fucking Marty," Donna lamented as she took another swirl of her beer.

"I'm going to have to talk to Al myself if Marty doesn't turn up," Donna said to herself.

"Did Al seem angry?" Donna inquired.

"No, but he was serious," Darin confessed.

Donna paused and held a stern stare on Darin for a brief but invasive moment.

"Where is Jimmy?" asked Darin, hoping to shift the focus away from himself.

"He's in jail; the idiot was caught drinking and driving again," Donna answered, with no perceivable regret.

"Want another beer?" Shannon said while grabbing two.

Donna didn't answer, but she did not have to, because Shannon pranced back from the fridge with another opened beer for her. She took the drink without acknowledging Shannon.

Darin noticed that Shannon was hoping to appease Donna and return to the festivities.

"You guys want to listen to Guns N' Roses?" Shannon inquired. Waiting for permission, Shannon swayed with the remnant of her feminine attributes. Donna looked at her and nodded with noticeable irritation.

Shannon scuttled back to the couch in her high heels and black, leather miniskirt. Donna poured another whiskey for Darin and herself. Darin took the drink by instinct rather than desire and downed the liquor, anticipating the warmness but disappointed by its waning effect of warmth. Donna got up and prodded her way to her room.

Shannon was leaning back, biting her lower lip, and staring at Darin. She looked at Donna's bedroom door and smiled. The part-time prostitute moved closer to Darin and placed her hand on his thigh.

Darin began to get excited as Shannon expected, but he remained closed to her advances. The licentious woman cared little for Darin's obvious predicament. Shannon knew that Donna was possessive of Darin and that he also found Shannon's advances difficult to resist.

"You don't want me?" Shannon whispered in Darin's ear. "I need you badly," Shannon continued.

Her advances were a hybrid of true lust and automatic conditioning. Her words felt scripted; yet they influenced men. She slept around a lot and must have told all her encounters the same thing. She never seemed genuine, but her sex was always available. Despite knowing that Shannon was a whore and that she wasn't very attractive, Darin always allowed her to play her part in this world.

He was lonely and awkward. He knew that Shannon only tried to come on to him when she was drinking at Donna's. It was a game to her, or a gift of affection that Shannon never learned to restrain for one man alone. Almost intoxicated more by her passions than by drink, Shannon poured a shot for Darin and handed it to him. "Here you go baby. Don't be so uptight," Shannon hummed with instinctive sexual powers.

Darin looked at her, took the shot, and lessened his emotional barrier. Shannon began to twirl the hair at the nape of his neck. Darin closed his eyes and focused on the light-but-charged gentle touch. He wished that Shannon's attraction was exclusive to himself and that this was his house. Donna would come out at any time and scold Shannon at best or thrash her at worst.

Donna's door opened, and a strange smell escaped her room. Shannon retreated like a lizard returning to a dark crevice. Darin remained stoic as stone and watched Donna leave her bedroom. Darin waited to see Donna's expression as she exited. Her countenance was altered by a hardening. She was not subdued by drink like she was when she had entered her room.

"How many times do I have to tell you to leave my nephew alone?" Donna lambasted Shannon.

"Ahh, it ain't nothin'," Shannon retorted.

Donna closed the distance and grabbed Shannon. The emancipated hooker became feral and ripped her wrists free of Donna's grasp.

"What the fuck are you doing, Donna?" Shannon screamed as she stood.

"Keep your filthy hands off of him," Donna raged, moving closer again.

Welcoming another assault, Shannon grabbed her purse and swung it at Donna. Donna reached back and slapped Shannon with a forceful blow. Shannon barely absorbed it and began to waiver. Donna then grabbed a handful of hair on the back of Shannon's head and beat her face repeatedly. The hooker's face dimmed, and her eyes rolled back. She was unconscious.

"She's my friend, Darin, not your slut," Donna panted. Darin was in shock but recovered some sense and knelt beside Shannon. He noticed that her chest was rising and falling; she was alive. He turned to face Donna, but she had retreated to her room.

Darin stared at Shannon, partly concerned and partly disappointed. She should have fought better than that, he thought to himself. Darin stood and walked to the sink, got a wet rag, and started patting her face with the cool cloth.

"Wake up," Darin whispered. He felt guilty for not checking on Donna, but he did not want Shannon to stay knocked out because he was worried that Donna might return unfulfilled with the results of her violence.

"Wake up, Shannon," Darin said as he shook her limp body.

She had never before looked so haggard to Darin. She was ugly; she was weak, and it disgusted him. Darin looked closely at her and noticed pockmarks and wrinkles that she had meticulously covered with heavy foundation. The sexual energy Shannon could animate had vanished. She was nothing more than a used vessel with a lingering ability to cast spells of intoxication. She was a whore. She was old before her time, and she had no power. Darin finally roused her. She began writhing and moaning. Her unconscious body was in pain. Darin got up, filled a glass of water, and returned to the brow-beaten tramp.

"Get her out of my house, Darin," Donna yelled through her bedroom door.

"I am," Darin returned almost inaudibly.

"Can you hear me?" Donna asked, with growing impatience.

"What's going on . . ." Shannon murmured through blunt trauma and intoxication.

"You need to go home now," Darin insisted while getting Shannon to her feet.

"Get that damn woman out of my house," Donna screamed from the doorway. Darin knew that he was running out of time, and he put his arms under Shannon's and lifted her to her wobbly feet. She had lost a heel, and Darin noticed that the polish had worn off her toenails. The red paint had flaked off, and her feet looked bony and large.

Her toes were long and augmented from years of being squashed in pointed shoes.

Darin wrestled her out the front door and rested her against the railing of the landing. He quickly went back inside to grab her heel and her purse. While scanning the living room, he made eye contact with Donna. She just looked at him. Her face exuded frustrated jealousy, concern, and pride in one glance. Darin pretended not to notice the mixture of strong feelings and returned to his hunt. He found her purse and clutched it as he continued hunting for the shoe. He saw it under the couch and got down on a knee to retrieve it.

Donna turned off the music, sat on the couch, and lit a cigarette. She knew that she was wrong, but wisdom was a true burden for the violent. She would not apologize or assist Darin. Shannon would be another victim of Donna's temper and never receive amends. Darin began to walk to the front door, and Donna said, "Get her home Darin and make sure she knows she's not welcome here again."

Darin nodded and walked out the door.

Shannon stood by bracing herself on the railing. A sobering clarity rested in her aura. Darin approached her gently. "I know, I heard her." Shannon spoke as she turned and faced him. The harlot had learned to maintain a particular dignity despite the many attacks she had endured. Her eyes were swollen, and her lip was fat. She smiled through the bruising and the blood. Her spirit was undefeated despite her flawed character. She held out her hand, and Darin handed her the shoe.

"Thanks, baby," Shannon said as she stood on one leg and slipped her foot into the four-inch heel.

Darin waited to hand her the purse, but she didn't wait. The years of walking the streets and taking abuse from the Johns had made her resilient. Shannon grabbed the purse, slung it on her shoulder, and walked towards the steps like a proud cat.

"I hope I see you around, Darin. You're not too bad of a fella," Shannon said with finality as she descended into the darkness.

"Bye, Shannon," Darin said while feeling resentment and regret.

He stood at the top of the steps and watched her walk away. He wanted to absorb this moment. How could he be so attracted and repulsed by the same woman for the same reasons? He wanted Shannon to be his girlfriend. He liked her feminine affections no matter how much she practiced them. He already missed her easy touch; yet he felt disdain for her weakness.

He lingered outside before entering the house. Donna had put on a Cream record to self-soothe. Looking at Donna gave Darin a mix of emotions. He felt owned and smothered by her dominant jealousy. Donna was an oasis of poison that staved off starvation. Darin walked in, looked at her, and felt anger and pity.

"I am going to bed," Darin said.

"What? You don't want to spend any time with me?" Donna responded, revealing need and anger.

Darin paused and then sat beside Donna. She moved closer to him and found a way to make herself small yet forceful. His body was repulsed by her advance, and his rigidness felt like rejection to her. She tried again to move past the blockade of instinct, but he tensed and slightly pulled away as he fought his usual surrender to Donna.

"You like that slut more than me?" Donna hissed as she abandoned her mockery of feminine enticement.

"I don't," said Darin.

"You piece of shit. You don't care about me?" Donna sneered as she stood sturdily.

Darin said nothing and lowered his head. Donna began whaling on Darin with powerful blows. Left, right, left . . . Darin took each hit with total acceptance. He was resigned to endure, to absorb her hate, her love. Then a strike stung, and the pain inhabited his total awareness as it drowned out every other hit. This pain connected to some emotion, and he suddenly missed his mother. He hated his mom for leaving him, and he hated this substitute for taking her place.

Darin stood. He was unaffected by Donna's continued barrage and grabbed her throat. She continued to land hard slaps on Darin as he grabbed her. Soon, she became aware that she was being strangled and attempted to pry his hands off her neck. Her wild eyes of rage changed to dim portals of terror. Resenting her panic, Darin squeezed harder. Flooded with shame and hate, Darin began to cry, and his grip constricted.

By the time he realized what he was doing, it was too late. He had engulfed the only woman in his world that embodied maternity. Darin let go of her lifeless form, and she fell to the floor. He sat on the couch and thought for a moment about going and retrieving Shannon. Now they could be together, and all would be well. He sat, and he looked at his aunt. He was still and understood that he would never see Donna again. He smiled through tears of grief.

Chapter 11

Every morning when Darin awoke, there was a moment of tranquility, the space between dreaming and waking. He did not remember killing Donna until he sat up and began to get dressed. He put on his pants and swiftly ascended the stairs from the basement. The bright morning light was a contrast to the dismal scene. There she was, stiff and cold. Around her were carpet stains, empty bottles, and a spilled ashtray.

He picked up her corpse and carried it to her bedroom. Touching her required him to shut down the repulsion he felt when his hands were on her lifeless body. All her malice, control, and dominating energies were gone.

"Don't worry; I'll clean the house," Darin said to the dead. He paused for a moment and half expected a response. He pulled back the blanket, laid her on the bed and covered her up.

He began cleaning up. Bottles went in the trash, ashes were vacuumed, and counters were wiped clean. When he had finished his work, he opened the fridge, and, to his surprise, there was half of a cold pepperoni pizza. Usually, Donna forbade Darin from eating her leftovers. Darin decided that she wouldn't miss one slice. Returning to the couch, he ate the food in the morning light. The sun was shining, and the heat was evaporating the dampness of the night before.

Perhaps Marty was back at work in Lake Oswego? he thought to himself. He filled a glass of water, drank it, and returned downstairs to finish dressing. After he put on his clothes, he went to the bathroom to brush his teeth. His reflection no longer made him uncomfortable. He was looking directly at himself, and the fullness of himself stared back. For the first time, he could recall that his own reflection was true.

Darin locked the door and hid the key. He bounced down the stairs, excited to find Marty and hopefully to see Melissa. As he approached Melissa's home, he could see that Marty's truck was not there. He was disappointed. If Marty was not at work or at home, and Al hadn't gotten ahold of him, then his location would not be discovered. Darin almost turned around to leave, but a longing to spy Melissia one more time got the better of him.

He remembered the first location on the side of the house where he had witnessed her. Slowly, he ambled down her driveway as if he lived there and made his way to that corner window. Hunching over as he neared, he allowed his sense of smell and hearing to dominate his awareness. Faint music came from the kitchen. He felt excitement. Perhaps she was dancing again, he thought to himself.

Slowly he lurched his head up, and there she was, but she was not alone. In the arms of a tall, handsome man, Darin found Melissa with her head on his chest. They were embracing, and the moment was serene. Darin felt a mixture of jealousy and admiration. He lost himself in voyeurism and malingered, losing the awareness that he was spying.

The man was dressed in business attire, and Darin assumed he would be leaving for work. He wanted to witness the final good-bye of the day, to absorb the found embrace to his memory bank, so that he could interpose himself later in his imaginations. The couple stopped swaying, and Melissa reached her arms around the neck of her man. Her eyes expressed passion, trust, and desire in one gaze. She was about to kiss her husband when she spotted Darin's visage in the lower corner of her window.

Gone was her glow, the tranquility of a lover's embrace destroyed by the discovery and terror of being watched. Melissa screamed, and the man twirled in response to his woman's fear. Darin was frozen in shock; he couldn't come to terms with the fact that he had been spotted. The man rushed for the door. Darin held Melissa's gaze for a moment longer and then abandoned his position.

Darin ran, and the man followed. Locked in pursuit, both men began to breathe heavily. The husband seemed to be catching up to Darin, but he slowed down when his penny loafers fell off. Darin was not a sprinter, but he was relentless in his endurance. Prodded on by fear and shame, Darin kept up his pace as the man, who was screaming, trailed off. "You better run; the police are coming!" the man screamed.

Without looking back, Darin pressed on and made his way to the bridge. Pushing through the overgrown branches that concealed his trail, he found his way to the overpass. The bums were all still passed out, and Darin continued to his enclave unnoticed. Then he began to cry. His tears escaped through his tight eyes. The emotion pushed through his effort to hold them in. As a failing dam reveals cracks by moistening walls, so did Darin's eyes. Once the tears pushed past the hard, closed eyelids, the dam broke, and Darin sobbed alone in the dark.

He remained still in the fetal position for a long time. He was overwhelmed. Had he forgotten his medication? Why was Melissa so frightened? Darin moaned in self-pity. He wanted to stay here forever, but hunger got the better of him after several hours, and he remembered the rest of the pizza in the fridge at home. After nightfall he could no longer resist the urge to eat something, and he slipped out of his crevice.

The vagrants were animated by cheap booze and barrel fires, but they were too intoxicated to notice Darin's passage through their encampment. As he made his way out, he noticed a new member of the derelicts—a young, blonde boy in his late teens, who was playing hand drums. The smile on the drummer was wild and energetic as his hands moved with precise rapidity. Darin liked this boy's music; it heightened his senses.

As Darin made his way through the tall, wet grasses and branches, the sound of the drums could still be heard creating a sense of enticement and magic. Like an indigenous hunter leaving the safety of his village to enter the wild, Darin pressed beyond the range of the percussion. At night, the park lost its serenity. During the day, families would stroll with their guard down; but at night, shadows darted, and figures loomed.

Something was different tonight. Darin had been at the park at night many times. Tonight, the darkness was heavy, and the lurking beings troubled him. It seemed as if they were now more aware of him. He felt their penetrating stares following him. Did they know that he killed his aunt? Were they coming for him? He quickly squelched his growing paranoia and moved with increased vigor to quiet his mind and escape the sensations.

Getting to a main road gave him comfort. The lights of the passing cars made him feel safer. By the highway he felt like just another person going home. Traffic was unusually busy that night, and he found it almost impossible to cross the street without running. As he darted across, a car honked and didn't slow down. It seemed that vicious operators inhabited the vehicles, and they were unconcerned about his life.

Making it across the street was an ordeal. He breathed heavily and considered returning to his shelter without stopping at home to eat. His hunger was powerful, and he was tired. The idea of getting home dominated his being. If he could just get to his room, everything would be all right. In his neighborhood now, he could relax a little. He would be home shortly and escape this feeling of dread.

As he neared the driveway, Darin noticed strange lights and commotion. He approached slowly with heightened alertness. Several police cars were haphazardly parked at his house. Flashlights darted back and forth. A police cruiser had its red and blue emergency lights on. Several of the officers were stringing yellow caution tape around the property.

Dumbfounded, Darin stood and observed the activity. Melissa and her husband had called the police. She must have known his full name. How did she know? Did Marty give it to her? A torrent of thoughts and questions flooded his mind as he watched authority figures seize and control the crime scene. Darin's home was lost. I am a murderer, Darin said to himself. He finally understood and internalized the full scope of his act.

His hunger was gone. He stood for a moment longer instinctually waiting for them to leave. But when he understood that he would never step foot inside his home again, he turned, put up his hood, and walked in the opposite direction of everything he knew. The rain started, but he maintained his pace. A few more police cars sped by, and he realized that he needed to get off the main roads.

When he got back to the park, he no longer felt watched or hunted. He felt absorbed and belonging. He was now a shadow of himself. Darkness was no longer a threat; light was. Without thought he made his way to the bridge. After clearing the brush, he noticed the drummer sitting alone by a campfire. Darin was wet and cold, so he sat next to the boy to dry off and warm himself.

He could see that the young hippie was happy to have company. The boy grinned widely, and Darin could see the top of the whites of his eyes. His hair was beginning to dread as a status symbol of freedom. He wore Converse shoes with pen drawings and holes, a hemp choker necklace, and loose-fitting clothes. Darin did not like him for some reason, but he was too wet to sleep in the nook under the bridge.

"Hey man . . . what's up?" inquired the dirty kid.

Darin sat a moment in silence searching for a response.

"Just trying to get dry," he finally responded.

"What are you doing out here?" asked the drummer.

"I live here now," he replied, warming his hands and avoiding eye contact.

The wide-eyed enthusiasm of the kid irritated Darin, especially because his eyes had a crazy look. The kid seemed to be too at ease with his environment and with him. Darin noticed his hands were like sandpaper, and his fingers were thick, filthy, and calloused. Darin could not distinguish whether he was drunk, high, or just weird.

"That's cool that you live here. I just got here and don't know where to sleep," said the kid.

"You might want to figure it out," said Darin, looking at a group of men off to the side of them.

The kid looked at them and whispered, "Yeah, I know those guys are no good."

Something about this lost hippie gave Darin a moment of empathy. He did not like him very much, but he somehow felt guilty and responsible for the youth. As they warmed themselves, the boy started to fiddle with his bongo drum. He gently and rhythmically engaged with the instrument; not to play music but to comfort himself.

"Where are you from?" Darin asked.

"I'm from Eugene, man," answered the kid as he played the instrument in an eight-stroke pattern.

"What's your name?" Darin reluctantly asked.

"It's Joshua, but I like to be called Kai. You seem legit. I don't normally tell people my real name," he answered.

Darin sat for a moment. He had never thought about giving himself a different name.

"Why do you like to be called Kai?" Darin asked.

"Dude, my parents named me Joshua from the Bible, and they are crazy. Plus, it's good to have a fake name when you're on the road!" Kai blurted as he performed upbeat on his drum.

"What's your name, bro?" asked Kai.

"It's Darin."

"Cool! That's a good name, man," Kai said with enthusiasm.

"If you're going to sleep here tonight, you should come with me to my spot," Darin said.

They stood and made their way up the embankment. Kai handed Darin a Bic lighter, and the two outcasts made their way into Darin's cave. Darin got curled up in his spot, and Kai situated himself as best he could with the remaining space. The enclave was warmer with two bodies, Darin quickly noticed. He was pleased with his decision to invite the dirty hippie.

As Darin was about to drift to sleep, Kai began to weep softly.

"Thank you for helping me out, man. Those guys started to give me the heebie-jeebies."

"They're not good," Darin answered flatly.

"Yeah, I could tell. Goodnight bro. Thanks," Kai said as he arrested his tears and gained control of his emotions. The pair slept like stray cats.

Chapter 12

When Darin opened his eyes, his face was swollen from dehydration and stress. He felt dirty and wanted to escape his own flesh. Two bodies in his burrow kept him warm but also made him sweat. Darin became acutely aware of how filthy and tired he really was. He couldn't move without waking Kai, and he didn't want to talk yet. So Darin just lay down for a moment, trying to overcome his nasty, uncomfortable feeling.

Soon he felt the urge to urinate. Kai was snoring, and Darin felt irritated by how relaxed the kid must be to sleep so loudly. Darin began to stir and wiggle his way out of the enclave. Kai didn't wake to Darin's rustling, and Darin made his way out of the hideout. The derelicts were strewn about, some still drinking and others passed out in unflattering ways.

Darin headed for a large bush to conceal himself while he went to the bathroom. His urine was brownish-yellow and burned a little. His fingernails were long and impacted with dirt. He felt ashamed to be holding his privates with such hands. He decided to get to the public bathroom at the park to wash up and drink some water. For a moment he hesitated and wondered if he should wake up Kai. After a brief period of thought, he decided that he was not responsible for the kid, and he would wake him after he washed up and got a drink.

The sun was out this morning, and several children were playing and being lazily watched by their parents. Darin felt a tinge of jealousy for the ease and joy that these people enjoyed. Pregnant women were being helped along by their doting husbands. Boys and girls were running back and forth, unhindered by fear or self-consciousness. The happiness and sunshine heightened his awareness of how he must look. Darin stormed to the latrine and lowered his pants.

Inside the restroom Darin felt better. The gray concrete and graffiti light dimly relaxed his growing agitation. Of course, the soap dispenser was empty; it was always empty. He took off his shirt and started to scrub his underarms. It felt good to have water on his body even if it was cool and there was no soap. The mirror was barely reflective and had strange and incomprehensible carvings on it.

He felt grateful that no parent and child entered the facility as he bathed. The cool water at least reduced some of the swelling in his face, and he was able to scrape out some of the dirt under his nails. He got his hair wet and combed it back with his hands. He then made his way to the fountain. The water did not rise out of the bubbler enough to drink without putting his mouth on the chrome hardware.

He would have found another location to quench his thirst had he. The sensation of cool water evaporated any revulsion Darin felt, and he drank his fill. Hunger returned, and this time he would retrieve his new friend. Darin walked back to the bridge and found

Kai still asleep.

"Wake up," Darin said as he shook Kai's shoulder.

The peaceful drummer stirred and rolled away from Darin.

"Kai . . . let's go get food," Darin said as he poked the kid. Kai stirred and looked around dumbfounded.

"What time is it, bro?" Kai responded as he rolled to face Darin.

He was beaming with youthful energy, and he was genuinely smiling.

"It's morning," Darin answered.

"Let me roll a smoke," Kia said as he fished out a pouch of tobacco and papers. "Do you want to roll one?" Kia asked as he deftly finished rolling and lighting his own cigarette.

"I'm good," Darin said.

Kai sat up in a relaxed manner and took long drags. The smoke filled the little cave and intermixed with the random sun beam. Kai looked fresh, and Darin was glad that the boy wasn't difficult to rouse. Kai jumped out of the crevasse with his backpack; the cigarette hung from his lips. After landing he whipped his long, blonde, dirty hair back and placed it in a ponytail. He then dug in a bag and revealed a bottle of Boone's Farm wine.

He took a long pull from the bottle and offered it to Darin. Instinctually, Darin reached to receive the bottle, but his senses got the better of him, and he lowered his hand.

"Maybe later. Let's get some bread," Darin said.

The two took off towards a bakery that Darin had discovered awhile back. Every morning, the unsold bread from the day before was given away or discarded. It was hard, but if it was placed near body heat or in an oven with some water drops, it was edible.

Luckily, they made it in time to retrieve some baguettes before the trash truck made its rounds.

"Dumpster diving!" Kai blurted with enthusiasm.

Darin only grabbed what he needed, but the hippie jumped in the dumpster and started rooting around.

"Just get what you need and let's go," urged Darin.

Kai popped up with his arms full and grinning ear to ear.

"Let's go!" Darin said with animation.

Kai wrestled his way out just in time to be scolded by an employee of the bakery.

"Hey! You can't be in there," yelled a soft-looking man with an apron and meticulously managed bread.

Kai sprinted off, dropping rolls as he clung to his pants and his baked varieties.

Darin walked briskly away but refused to run from a dandy. The pursuer slowed his pace when he realized that Darin was not fleeing in fear. The baker with the styled facial hair irritated Darin, and he felt the courage to attack him. The "artisan maker" was nothing more than a minimum wage earner. Darin stopped walking away for a moment and turned to look at the baker.

"You can't be doing that," said the employee.

"Why not?" replied Darin through gritted teeth.

"It's illegal!" cried the baker.

"I'm hungry," replied Darin.

Something switched in the dough boy, and he relented. Maybe it was Darin's brutal countenance, or maybe it was the reality that hunger trumped the law.

"Alright, just get out of here please," said the bearded man.

Darin turned and walked away, placing the baked goods under his recently cleaned armpit.

Back at the park he caught up with Kai. The kid was sitting in the grass surrounded by inedible baked goods.

"How am I supposed to eat this?" the drummer said as he knocked two pieces of bread on his head in a rhythm.

Darin pulled his baguette from under his shirt and took a bite. The drummer laughed and started shoving all the plundered bread under his shirt. "Yo-ho-ho and a bottle of rum!" the kid sang as he laughed to himself.

Darin sat down and started to eat.

Maybe it was the sun; maybe it was the bread; it could have even been the small victory shared with his new friend. Darin smiled and ate his food with contentment. The two young men forgot they were vagrants and had a picnic of rolls, baguettes, and brioches. After they had eaten, and the sun grew hotter, they made their way back to the bridge.

The duo sat under the bridge; digestion was making them sluggish. Kai pulled out his bottle and tobacco and started drinking and smoking. Darin picked up a stick and doodled in the dirt with it. There they sat with nothing more to do, and no place to be. It was still morning.

"Why did you leave Eugene?" Darin asked with genuine interest.

"Ah, man, my pops got super religious and joined this church," Kai said, while fiddling with the label on his wine.

"What's wrong with that?" Darin continued.

"It was cool for a while, but then they started getting real controlling. My mom wasn't allowed to cut her hair, and my dad started getting wacky ideas. The main guy started telling everyone that the end was near and that to be good with God, we had to leave our house and move to his property," Kai explained.

Darin nodded, not satisfied.

"Yeah, man; so after we moved there, the guy starts telling everyone that he needs more wives and stuff like that. So my pops and mom agree to let him marry my little sister. I was not about that man, and I told my pops," Kai continued.

"So what happened?" Darin pressed.

"Dude, I got into it with my pops bad, and he told me to get lost. My sister and mom agreed with him! I couldn't believe it, bro, and I left. They are in a cult for sure." Kai took another strong pull of his Boone's Farm until it was emptied.

"You gonna go back?" Darin questioned.

"Nah, bro . . . can't. The main guy kicked me out and said that I should honor my father and mother. That's it. I'm out," Kai said with finality. "What about you, man?" Kai asked, relieved to turn the focus off himself.

"I got into a fight with my aunt, and I can't go home either," Darin said.

"What did y'all get in a mix-up about, bro?" Kai asked.

"I liked a girl that didn't want to be with me," Darin explained.

"Bummer, bro, Romeo and Juliet!" Kai said, with a teasing tone.

Darin blushed a little and became visibly aggravated.

"Ah, I'm just joshing ya," Kai said, with a grin that revealed yellow teeth. "Let's go see this babe," Kai said as he threw his empty bottle against a concrete bridge pillar.

Shannon lived in the trailer park. Darin had been thinking about her since the night Donna hurt her. He had never been to her house before, but he knew what she drove. Shannon only came to their house. Darin understood why when he found her trailer. There were three cars in her driveway. Her own, an empty Ford pickup truck, and a sedan with a man sitting in the driver's seat exhibiting visible anxiety.

She was working. Darin was disappointed because he felt embarrassed in front of Kai. The young musician was paying attention to details, and he was amused by the surroundings.

"Bro . . . look at that place; they got everything in their yard," Kai said, more to himself than Darin.

Darin didn't look. He was too busy looking at the john in the car. He would rather watch someone waiting to sleep with Shannon than think about her having intercourse this very moment. All that man had to do was pay a few bucks, and he could violate her. It didn't matter if he was funny, strong, or interesting; he just needed cash. He didn't harbor jealousy; he was irritated.

Hookers and broken men had provided emotional support for each other since the beginning of time. The woman needed a male figure that she could trust, and the man needed a woman that could nurture him without being provided for. A large man exited the trailer looking fresh and pleased with himself. He walked like a bull, and his presence made the man in the car shrink. The large man put his trucker hat on, shot a smirk at the other fellow, and jumped in his truck. The old Ford started on the first turn of the key and rumbled with power.

He backed out of the driveway and was gone. The other man sat up and turned his full attention to the front door. Darin thought about approaching and telling him to get lost. He knew that Shannon would be pissed and perhaps not talk to him if he did; so he sat on the curb and continued to watch. After a tense intermission, the door opened, and Shannon emerged wearing a short Asian-looking robe. It was pale green with contorted dragons and floral patterns.

The man got out of the car; he was skinny, bald, and eager. Darin hated him. The man that left was at least capable, deserving of a woman. This man was gross, needy, and weak. Darin could barely keep his pride contained.

"Hey, man, what's your old lady doing?" Kai said with visible jest. "I thought this was your girl, bro." the kid continued.

"She is not my girl, but she could have been," Darin snapped.

"She is that dude's girl now," Kai said, tapping on the curb like a drum. Darin turned to him with a complete shift in bearing. Kai looked him in the eyes and submitted.

"Sorry, man," Kai said, cowed.

The two sat in silence, and Darin endured waiting for the bald little man to finish his bought time. Shannon lived close to Marty's trailer, and Darin took note that Marty's truck was still missing. Al must have got him, Darin thought out loud.

"Got who, bro?" Kai asked with newly restored humility.

Darin looked at Kai and was shocked that the kid had heard him.

"What?" Darin said, looking at Kai with visible irritation.

"Uh . . . you said Al must have got him. Got who?" Kai reiterated.

"My boss went missing a few days back, and I think he owed this guy named Al some money."

"That's heavy, man," Kai said back.

Darin waited for more questions, but the kid had already moved on and was laughing at a woman that was trying to get her dog to come back in the trailer.

"Hahaha, look over there, man. That dog is stressing that lady out!" Kai said, very amused. "I love trailer parks; real shit, man," Kai said, smiling.

Darin kept his eyes on Shannon's door. What are they doing? It's been twenty minutes, Darin thought. He stood, responding to an urge to go and look through a window. He started walking towards the trailer, and the drummer snapped up and followed. As the duo approached, the front door opened, and Shannon led the wimpish little man out. She had her arm on his back, and the man seemed embarrassed or ashamed. Shannon patted him a few more times and directed him to his car.

The man complied and got in his compact car and started it. He sat there for a moment looking at Shannon; she had lit a cigarette and was leaning on the door frame. She waved with her fingers, somehow being caring and direct in one small gesture. Darin moved toward her as the man backed out of the driveway. Their eyes met, and the little man's rageful little portals were full of possessiveness.

Darin broke contact and greeted Shannon. The sedan sped off aggressively, but Darin was unconcerned. Shannon did not look pleased to see Darin.

"What are you doing here?" She asked, with genuine concern

and fear.

Kai's smile faded, and he stepped back. Darin paused and moved a little closer.

"I came to see if you were alright," Darin proclaimed.

"Oh, I'm fine, but they found Donna, you know?" Shannon answered by playing the role of the hardened hooker.

Darin froze. She knew. He had hoped that everyone would have thought that Donna had overdosed or had an accident.

"The cops are looking for you, Darin," Shannon said, devoid of any familiar compassion.

Darin lowered his head.

He thought for a moment and then looked up. "I just wanted to know if you were ok," Darin said as a statement and a question.

"I'm fine, honey, but you better get out of here before someone calls the police. Don't come back either," Shannon said as she flicked her cigarette over the railing.

"Let's go, Darin" Kai blurted.

Darin was unresponsive for a moment. He wished he had not killed Donna; he wished that it was all a dream. His eyes watered, and he began to shake with overwhelming emotion.

"I'm sorry," Darin said.

"You gotta go now," Shannon said with finality.

Darin turned and walked off the porch stairs.

"What was that, man?" Kai said with bewilderment "Did you kill someone?"

"No!" Darin shouted.

"That lady sure thinks you did," Kai said with concern.

"It's a misunderstanding; it's not true," Darin said as panic began to surface. He made his way back to the bridge, and the hippie followed but at a bit of a distance. Kai was upset by the situation. He was following Darin out of a mixture of instinct, or, possibly, stupidity.

Chapter 13

The pair made it to the bridge late in the afternoon. The campsite was empty except for the two young men. Darin squatted on his haunches with a stick that he used to poke at the embers of a dying fire. Kai stayed standing, keeping a noticeable distance from Darin. They both knew that the other knew, but neither wanted to let the other know. The shame of being a murderer discovered for what he really was could be even worse than realizing that a mate was indeed a killer.

Kai grabbed his backpack out of Darin's den. He paused and then spoke. "Man, thank you for hooking me up with a place to stay last night."

"You're leaving?" Darin asked.

"Yeah, man, it's all pretty heavy stuff, and I don't want to be involved," the hippie said as he clutched his bag.

"I didn't kill her," Darin said, raising his head and attempting to smile.

"Of course, bro, but, still, I better get on my way," Kai said with gentleness.

"Are you going to tell anyone where I am?" Darin asked, standing coiled.

"Why would I do that, man? It's none of my business," said the drummer with growing alarm.

Darin lunged at the kid, but Kai's reflexes were too fast. The kid side-stepped Darin and darted away. Darin gave chase but soon realized that he would not be able to catch him. Darin did not want to kill Kai, but he did not want to let him go either. He returned to the encampment and sat there feeling defeated.

Darin remembered being a boy in school before his mother died. The other boys would tease him relentlessly. He wanted so much to be a part of the group, but every attempt to gain acceptance ended in ridicule or deep embarrassment. Once a boy had told Darin that if he stole some Smurf figurines from the teacher's desk, then he would be Darin's best friend. The teacher had confiscated them earlier in the year from a group of boys.

Excited for an opportunity to earn friends, Darin did as he was asked. At the next recess, Darin hid in the back of the classroom as they roared out in a pandemonium. He searched the teacher's drawer and quickly discovered the toys. He took all of them and placed them in his own desk cubby. Pleased with himself, he then slipped outside to join the other kids. The ringleader ran up to him and asked if he had found the Smurfs. Darin said that he had, and then the boy told the rest of the group what Darin had done.

Instead of being excited, the boys were teasing and threatening.

"You're going to get in trouble," said one boy.

"That's detention for sure," said another.

When the kid who had orchestrated the operation realized that his group did not support the theft, he turned on Darin.

"How could you do something so stupid?" said the boy as he and the others crowded in closer.

The group ran off, leaving Darin with tremendous fear and a sense of rejection. Soon he realized that the boys had told the teacher what he'd done. The instructor approached Darin and asked him if he had been in her desk. Realizing that a lie would offer no protection, he reluctantly admitted that he had.

Darin tried to tell her that the other boy had asked him to do it. She didn't want to hear excuses. They entered the classroom and went to his desk. The teacher told him to show her the toys. Darin noticed that the group of boys were crowded together by the window and watching. With an angry tone the teacher repeated herself and commanded Darin to open it now.

He did as he was told, and there were the Smurfs. The onlooking boys howled in excitement. The teacher grabbed his arm and escorted him from the classroom to the principal's office. Darin got swatted and expelled for three days. His mother beat him when he got home, and the rest of the boys in the class avoided him for the rest of the year.

* * *

He did not want to hurt Kai, but he didn't want to be betrayed. If he saw the kid again somewhere, he would have to keep him quiet. Night came on faster than normal it seemed. The ghastly men filtered into the camp. They made Darin uncomfortable, so he retreated to his nook. They laughed but kept away from him.

He lay alone in the darkness. Anxiety had turned to terror, and terror had turned to despair. He knew he would be discovered, but where could he go? As the night wore on, his feeling of desperation transformed into acceptance. He was a murderer. He had no one to turn to, and he deserved any punishment that he got. In this acceptance he no longer feared being restrained or discovered.

Darin lay in darkness of the night and his soul. Commotion started in the camp, and Darin knew it was the police. Bums yelled as the cops apprehended and questioned them.

"Have you seen a young man with dark hair and pale skin?" a familiar voice questioned. Most of the vagrants were too intoxicated to be of any use.

"Here it is," yelled a voice after a bright light illuminated the entrance to Darin's cave.

Darin popped out and made a run for it. He quickly realized that several officers were surrounding him, and he darted for the biggest gap he could find. There was a heavy thud on the ground, and Darin lost his breath. Then there was a struggle. One of the police officers smashed Darin's head with his heavy-duty Maglite. Others jumped on him and wrestled his arms behind his back.

Darin resisted, and the familiar voice cut through to him. "If you keep resisting, I'll break your arm," said Officer Caliban.

Darin eyes grew wide with shock, and he flailed with greater energy. True to his word, Caliban levered Darin's arm and broke his shoulder. The pain was great, and Darin succumbed to the weight of the men. Caliban put handcuffs on Darin with extreme tightness. Darin winced in pain, and he heard the officers laugh.

The figures moved toward him. Darin could not see their faces because of the blinging, powerful Maglites. Their radios continued to squawk as the officers hoisted him to his feet. Darin could see some of the homeless men watching the arrested him with amusement while the others just passed out again. Caliban slid his arm under Darin causing immense pain as he guided his prisoner out of the camp.

Another officer clicked the radio and informed dispatch that Darin had been apprehended. The officers laughed and exchanged quick jokes as they made their way through the dark forest to the main park trail. As they continued, Darin felt like a hero. He did not know why, but he felt like a good person. Caliban noticed him smiling and levered harder. Darin shrieked in sharp, overwhelming agony and smiled no more.

When the group reached the cars, Caliban hesitated to put Darin in the back seat. The other officers got in their cars and started to leave. Once Caliban had Darin to himself, the beating started. He took out his night stick and beat the back of Darin's thighs until he fell. With each blow Darin received, the pain grew less impactful.

"I see you still like hurting women," Caliban grunted between strikes. "I knew you were a piece of shit the first time I arrested you," Caliban continued.

Darin absorbed each blow like a heavy bag being wailed on by a hard puncher. Caliban grew infuriated by Darin's lack of response and began to hit him harder with growing ferocity. Caliban's partner blurted out that he was going to kill him. Caliban was intoxicated with fury and paid no heed to his partner. He began kicking him with his issued black leather boots. Darin started to spit blood and to fade out of consciousness.

"That's enough. That's enough!" yelled the other officer as

he grabbed Caliban and pulled him away. Darin smiled at Caliban through blood and dirt.

"Don't piss yourself in my car again," Caliban said as the other officer began to pick him up.

"Let me put him in the cruiser now. I can't lose this job because you lose your shit," said the other officer.

Caliban said nothing but did not hinder the officer as he picked up Darin and placed him in the back of the patrol car. The two men got in the car, radioed an update, and began driving. Darin struggled to stay alert, but he grew weak. The hum of the cruiser was too much for him, and he lost awareness.

Darin woke up in a hospital bed. He had no idea how long he had been in the medical center. The lights were bright, and the smell of bleach overwhelmed him. He wanted to leave, to eat, and to know if he was okay. His body ached, and he had a tube coming out of the back of his hand. The monitor to his left seemed to indicate that his heart was fine.

A nurse appeared not long after he woke up. She avoided eye contact, looked at his saline bag, checked the monitor, and made a note on her clipboard.

"Is everything all right?" Darin asked. It was difficult to speak.

The nurse tried to ignore him by hiding behind her uniform and duties. Darin could see that she had heard him but was pretending that he was incomprehensible. With more effort Darin tried again.

"Am I going to be okay, ma'am?" he repeated with more force.

"The doctor will be with you shortly to answer questions," replied the nurse.

Darin gave up on the woman. All institution workers were

like little worker bees, going to and fro with little identity or concern for others outside of their job duties.

The nurse left, and Darin was glad. She only reminded him of how alone he felt. He tried to recollect how he had gotten to the hospital. He could remember the officer beating him, but he did not understand why. Maybe I did something wrong. Maybe they are scared, Darin thought. He watched the staff rush around wishing he could get up.

Darin was handcuffed to the hospital bed, but this time the cuffs were not too tight, and he was pleased about that. He noticed a bathroom and realized that he didn't need to use it. He thought that was strange because he always had to go when he woke up. With his free hand he reached down to his crotch instinctually and felt a tube coming out of his penis.

Darin tugged at it, but the sensation hurt too much to pull it completely out. He continued his search and realized that there was a bag filled with urine at the end of the tube. Darin began to feel rage. He was trapped, tubed, and no one was explaining anything to him. He closed his eyes tightly, and tears pushed through his eyelids once more. He did not want to cry, but what he wanted mattered little to others or himself.

He composed himself and waited. A long time passed before the doctor arrived. The medical professional was not alone, but the other people with the doctor remained by the door.

"How are you feeling, Mr. Brennan?" the tall, unemotive, meticulously groomed man asked.

"I dunno," answered Darin.

The two stared at each other for a moment, and Darin could

see that the doctor was disgusted with him.

"You have two broken ribs with a skull fracture with some internal bleeding," announced the tall man in white.

Darin just continued to look at him.

"You were severely hurt while resisting arrest," the doctor blurted. Darin was shocked by his lack of a professional filter.

Darin accepted what the man told him. He made no excuses.

"Will I be okay?" Darin asked.

"You will recover, but it will take some time," answered the doctor with a practiced smile. "The nurses will take care of you, and you can push that buzzer if you need anything," said the tall medical man.

Then the doctor closed his aluminum clipboard and exited the room. Two of the others with him cast final glances and whispered among themselves as they followed the doctor. Darin hated them. He was so frustrated by their presence that he forgot to ask about the tube stuck in his genitals. He took a big sigh and went inside himself, an internal, bracing, and soothing space of indifference and thoughtlessness.

The nurses emptied his urine bag, checked his pulse, administered medications, and helped him go to the toilet when he had to defecate. Time went by—a week or two—Darin could not be sure. The days and nights melded together, and the only entertainment available to him was a Bible. He tried to read it, but he found it extremely hard to comprehend. No one had ever told him about God let alone anything about the Bible.

Darin felt a strange attraction to the book, but the words were small, and he could not read very well. He got as far as the story of Cain and Abel where God warns Cain about sin.

"If you do what is right, will you not be accepted? But if you do not do what is right, sin is crouching at your door; it desires to have you, but you must rule over it."—Genesis 4:7

Had "sin" devoured him? Darin felt a great burden; he was a murderer. He did not know God. No one had ever told him about the Bible, or about sin. He closed the Gideon Bible and placed it back in the drawer where he had discovered it. Maybe I will read more tomorrow, he thought.

Chapter 14

Tomorrow never came. Police officers arrived to take Darin to jail where he would await trial. His body had healed enough, and the hospital needed the bed. No one said farewell as he was escorted out of the medical facility. It was too painful for him to walk, so he was pushed in a wheelchair. The damage to his legs had not seemed to fully recover.

Darin was happy to leave the hospital. He did not like being cared for by people that maintained a professional mask. He could tell they despised him and detested waiting on him. It was a relief to be in the care of people that openly expressed disdain. Pretense was difficult to bear when there was no way for redemption.

The officers that were transporting him acted like he wasn't even there. They commanded him to sit or move, and he did. Then they continued their discussion about a party they went to over the weekend. Darin liked being treated as an object. He did not have to interpret, verbally respond, or pretend. He was a prisoner, and they were his guards. Simple and true.

Riding in the car was pleasant. The day was bright, and his mood was content. Just like the day Donna had picked him up as a child. The interludes between places were a gift, a glimpse of other worlds. Darin smiled as the officers cracked jokes and rehashed romantic escapades. He felt like he belonged, like he had a place. The officer driving heard him giggle and looked in the rearview mirror. Darin looked at him and could see that the policeman was surprised Darin was engaged with his stories of sexual conquest.

The two officers ended their banter and drove in silence after reporting their proximity to arrival. Darin laughed to himself, only looking away from the officer's mirror after the sergeant first broke eye contact. Everything seemed better. Darin liked the pain of his injuries, the appropriate tightness of his restraints, and the casual speed of the vehicle.

They got to the jail, and Darin hardly noticed the fences and barbed wires. He wanted to walk and take in the sunshine. His only regret was how close to the front door the officer had parked. As the officers assisted Darin out of the car, he took a deep breath, like a diver getting ready to make a descent. The warmth of the sun seemed to offer him more in this moment than ever before. Like the last kiss of a departing mother.

Once he got inside, it was business as usual for the guards. They were neither rude nor polite. Just efficient; alert but not interested. Darin, stripped and naked, had his body scanned by reluctant inspectors, and was given a green jumpsuit. He was glad to have the issued clothes because wearing his old garments made him feel dirty after his body was cleaned in the hospital.

The other men in jail acted strange to Darin. Some were trying to be in charge; some were keeping to themselves. For the men going to prison, jail was where they started trying to establish a reputation as somebody not to mess with. The men that hoped for freedom tried to keep a low profile. Pending fates had a strange way of altering current behavior even for the incarcerated.

Darin didn't understand what was going to happen to him. He was pretty sure that prison was his fate. Some of the men in jail seemed to be wise concerning the justice system. Darin wondered how such men ended up behind iron to begin with. Hope and despair guarded the men in jail as much as the locks and guards. He decided to relinquish hope and accept despair. Perhaps he would grow to like it as much as apple pie instead of berry pie.

Darin mostly kept to himself. He had been told that a public defender would come to see him soon, and it would be best if there were no disciplinary issues prior to his getting an appointed lawyer. Darin felt gratitude that he was being issued legal counsel. He estimated that a lawyer could help him understand the legal process.

Several days went by, perhaps even weeks. His relationship to time was growing strange after the murder. He could sit in a cell alone for hours, and it would only feel like minutes. Then he could hardly stand the monotonous passage of time. His very skin was a prison. Darin learned that if he kept his focus on the moment, time would lose its total power.

The day came when he met his lawyer. The man was thin, balding, and had slender, soft fingers. Darin hated him. The public defender was visibly anxious and exuded an air of contained vindictiveness. When Darin approached the man, who was sitting at a table, he glanced up without a smile and looked at the chair across from him. Darin understood that was his invitation to sit.

"My name is Mr. Bauer, and I have been appointed as your

public defender," the lawyer said without looking into Darin 's eyes. Darin nodded with crossed arms. "I see you are being charged with second-degree murder, aggravated assault, and resisting a peace officer," said Mr. Bauer with dimly concealed repulsion.

"What is second degree?" Darin asked.

"It means, Mr. Brennan, that you took the life of another person without planning it in advance. It's a very serious charge," Mr. Bauer said with growing confidence.

Darin noticed that hearing his last name used most likely indicated that he would have little control on the outcome of all this. Last names were used to direct a command at you or to condemn. Police officers, lawyers, doctors, and teachers used last names like a shock collar on a spirited dog. Darin despised the little official even more as they continued their part in the state's masquerade.

"I did not plan to kill my aunt. That is true. But she hurt me many times," Darin replied.

"How did your caretaker hurt you?" asked Mr. Bauer with disbelief.

"She would make me sleep with her; she would beat me," Darin said this out loud for the first time in his life.

Something about revealing his abuse made Darin feel weak and dishonest. The lawyer looked at him with shrewd disbelief. Darin began to wonder if he had wanted Donna to treat him as she did. He could have resisted; he could have run away. Why didn't he do something different? Darin felt like a liar, a fake, a murderer.

"You're a very strong-looking young man, Mr. Brennan. It's going to be difficult to convince a judge, let alone a jury, that you were being abused by an older woman that was your caretaker," the waif of a man informed Darin.

Darin felt estranged from reality. Donna was right all along. No one cared about him. He was useless, a burden. He was lucky to have had his aunt. He almost missed her. Up until this moment, Darin had thought of himself as misunderstood or as an outsider. Right now, he felt like a wolf in a trap. Beasts don't know they are wild things that must be hunted and contained until they are caught and measured by the laws and institutions of the men that learned how to hide their aggression.

"What happens now?" Darin asked.

"The prosecutor has offered a plea deal. Plead guilty to second degree murder, and the state will drop the other charges. You will then face life in prison, with a minimum of twenty years," said the lawyer.

Darin thought for a moment and decided that getting two charges dropped sounded good. He did not want to be guilty of murder, but he did take Donna's life with his own hands. He was even grateful that he was being offered such a fair deal. He wanted all this to be over. He wanted to stop running, answering questions, and trying to explain things. Life in prison sounded horrible, but twenty years felt like a fair sentence for murder. "That sounds good," Darin said.

The thin lawyer looked pleased, and he explained to Darin how the process would go. He would inform the prosecutor and the judge about Darin accepting the plea, and then the judge would administer sentencing. After that, Darin would start his time in a maximum state penitentiary. The lawyer explained more, but it mattered little to Darin.

For the first time since he had arrived at jail, Darin felt hungry and curious about what would be served for lunch. He waited in line and was served green beans, mac & cheese, sliced ham, and a pint of milk. His body yearned for the food. He made his way to an open seat and ate with satisfaction. When he finished his food, he went to his bunk and slept.

Time carried on in the same manner. He would mark his days by meals. He would eat, sleep, and eat. He started to gain weight, but the extra girth made him feel comfortable. Something about the added weight made him feel whole and healthy. His routine was only disturbed by the other criminals causing problems for the guards. When unrest altered the sequence, Darin would just stay in his cell and sleep. His life was reduced to eating, sleeping, and waiting.

The day came that Darin was informed he would be transported to court to be sentenced. Now that he had established a pattern of familiarity, the impending trip caused some anxiety. He took extra time in the showers to groom himself as best he could. His hair was longer now, and his uniform fit snugly. He was a bit embarrassed to be presented to a judge in a tight, green jumpsuit with long hair.

The ride in the van offered little light and voyeurism. He was handcuffed and sat far away from the front window. The back window was caged, and he couldn't make out much because the window was too far away. This disturbed Darin because these minor jaunts were his only insight to the world of people that he would never know.

When they arrived at the court, his public defender was not there. The clerk informed him that Mr. Bauer was running late but would be there in time for sentencing. Darin was seated on a bench in the hallway of the courthouse. The guards towered over him. They were relaxed but professional. Their usual conversation was altered due to the guards being on 'official' duty.

Darin felt invisible, like a mandatory observer of himself. He wondered why this formality had to be acted out. He had already accepted the plea. The court could have filed a paper and been done with him. Must the mockery continue? What more did they need from him? The tension of the day gave Darin gas, and he held it in, causing him minor distress.

The bloating combined with the cleanliness of the government building made Darin feel even more out of place. He did not belong here. This place was not for him, but rather for the bureaucrats the citizens, the officials. Darin hated those people, their lives, their roles, and their need for officiality. He hung his head and tried to escape in thought.

When Mr. Bauer arrived, he was perspiring and seemed disorganized.

"Are you ready?" he asked.

"Yes, are you?" Darin fired back.

Mr. Bauer smiled with poorly veiled contempt and nodded that he was ready. The guards lifted Darin to his feet and guided him to the courtroom. Darin had expected more out of the judge and the proceedings. Everything seemed childish and silly. The judge looked like a character out of a story with his double chin and black robe.

The typist was old and wore large, framed glasses, and she had a confetti chain. The guard for the judge was a large, black man, who seemed too comfortable with observing peoples' demise. Mr. Bauer's visible anxiety now greatly angered Darin. This little man has no ability or confidence, Darin thought. He is just another actor in this performance.

"All rise," announced the bailiff.

The staff roused. There was no one else at the hearing. No witnesses, no journalists, and no family. Formalities were expressed, and they were seated. The judge asked the prosecutor's office and the public defender if the plea had been accepted. He then went on to inform the court of the crime and the maximum penalty.

"I hereby sentence you, Mr. Brennan, to life in prison without the possibility of parole," bellowed the judge as the typist banged and the gavel fell.

The bailiff smirked, and the guards stood Darin on his feet once more. Mr. Bauer scurried off, and Darin was escorted out of the courtroom, the building, and back into the van. He felt swept away. He had heard nothing except the sentencing. He had seen in movies that the defendant gets a final word, but that never came. Maybe it did, but he missed it. Now he urgently had to go to the bathroom, but he was already in the van being transported to the state penitentiary in Salem.

He could hardly think because his thoughts were on holding his waste. The ride down to Salem from Portland was miserable. Darin was expressly focused on not soiling himself. Maybe he should ask the guards to let him use a rest stop? Maybe he could hold it and go when they got to the state prison? With each minute, the need grew until Darin was compelled to ask them to stop.

"I have to go to the bathroom," Darin yelled from the back of the van.

"We can't stop. You have to hold it," yelled back the passenger guard without facing Darin.

"I have to go right now!" Darin grimaced as he yelled again.

"Too fucking bad, scumbag," yelled the guard, who this time faced him with aggression.

Darin could see that the men would not stop and that he had to hold it or shit himself. The idea of arriving in prison with feces loaded in his pants was not an option. He committed himself to hold it at all costs. In this manner, Darin made his trip from sentencing to prison.

Chapter 15

When Darin arrived at the state penitentiary, the guards allowed him to use the bathroom before starting official in-processing. The dread of facing life in prison and being a new prisoner was displaced by the natural urgency of needing to relieve himself. He was grateful to be able to use the toilet. Relief of human emergencies is its own joy, he thought. Darin was now ready to face the system that would own him.

As the guards issued his clothes, Darin was pleased that the green uniform would be traded for bland, regular clothes like jeans, T-shirts, and a sweater. Prison was already feeling better than county jail. As he made his way to his cell, some of the other inmates were catcalling. Darin felt naked and weak by the hyperfocused attention. Some of the men felt lust, and some laughed at the mockery. Others looked through Darin to sense what kind of man he was.

He walked with his head up, but not too high. He kept his eyes facing ahead and did not show emotion. Some of the men at the county had told Darin that the first few weeks of being in prison would set the tone for years. Part of him wanted to perform well, and another part of him wanted the violence that would come. These men, these evil energies encased in concrete and iron, would be an outlet for his rage.

The guard brought him to his cell. Darin made eye contact with his new cellie and felt anxiety. The prisoner smiled at Darin with a mixture of excitement and greed. Darin sighed. He had hoped that his cellmate would be weak, or small. Instead, he was cast into a cage with a man that exuded lust and hate.

"Play nice, Papa Bear," said the guard with uncomfortable amusement. Papa Bear kept his eyes on Darin without acknowledging the guard's half-hearted command. Darin braced himself and crossed the threshold while clutching his issued items. The guard chuckled a little more and then shut the door. Darin did not bother to turn to the guard. He knew that no sympathy or protection would come from the little man who was unable to fill out his uniform. Darin thought that the prisoners and the guards were the same except some were paid and got time off.

There was an awkward moment where Darin and Papa Bear looked at each other without speaking. Darin looked at the bunks which both had items on them. He expected the large man to tell him which bed would be his. Papa Bear was balding and wore a stained wife-beater. He simply stood there and waited.

"Which bunk is yours?" asked Darin.

"Both of them," said Papa Bear.

Darin threw down his clothes and stood ready for combat. Papa Bear was not expecting this kind of reaction. Based on Darin's size and demeanor, Papa Bear was hoping to terrorize his new guest. Darin was not having it. He had committed to himself prior to arrival that he would rather die than be humiliated and dominated by another man.

"Slow down, Hair Trigger, I'm just fucking with you," said Papa Bear.

Darin was shaking, not from fear but from unused adrenaline. He wanted to grab the man's thick neck and shove his thumbs in his eyes. Darin had visualized his attack with such clarity that it took a few moments to compose himself. He almost attacked him anyway to relieve the pressure of rage in his body. Papa Bear giggled and disengaged.

The large man cleared his articles off the top bunk and gestured to Darin that the top bed would be his. Darin could see that Papa Bear was a homosexual who liked that tension of the line between fear and violence.

"Alright," said Darin. He picked up his bundle of issued items and placed them on the foot of the bed.

"What are you locked up for?" Papa Bear asked in a teasing manner.

"Murder," said Darin.

"Well then you're in the right place," Papa Bear said with a smile.

The two men awkwardly shared the cell as Papa Bear listed his rules.

"Don't touch my stuff; stay out of my drawers; and keep the toilet clean," Papa Bear explained. Darin nodded in agreement.

"Do you smoke?" Papa Bear asked.

"No," said Darin.

"Good, because I don't like smoke. No smoking in this cell,"

Papa Bear continued.

After the ground rules were laid out, Darin climbed on his bunk and shut his eyes. I might have to kill this man, he thought to himself. As the hours ticked away, the impending feeling of conflict subsided, and Darin began to relax. A few more hours went by, and then it was chow time.

The men made their way to the cafeteria, and Darin learned the new system. He got his food and made his way to a table. He sat down next to a skinny man with tattoos and a short fat man with glasses. The three men ate in silence until the tattooed man began to speak. "Papa Bear is a bad first cellie," said the man without looking at Darin.

Darin looked at the man, but the man did not look back.

"Ain't that right 4.0?" the man said while looking at the short man in glasses.

The man called '4.0' laughed nervously and agreed. "Yeah, boy, you best watch that ass," Tattoo said as he smiled to himself and ate his greens.

Darin just ate; he did not ask questions. He knew what they meant. Papa Bear walked by, casting looks at Darin. He then sat with some other large men. Darin watched him whisper to the other men, and they all turned to him and sneered. Darin looked back at his food and continued to eat. "There you go, son," said Tattoo.

"Seriously, you need to watch your back," uttered 4.0.

Darin decided that he would kill Papa Bear or any other man that tried to rape him. If attackers got past his vigil, and he couldn't fight them off, he would find a way to seek revenge at the first opportunity. Darin's fear and anxiety abated when he made this vow to himself once more. He enjoyed his food and appreciated the company and warnings from Tattoo and 4.0.

The brief interlude called lunch was over, and the three men brought their trays back to the kitchen to be stacked for cleaning. The large men that were sitting with Papa Bear came within inches of Darin at the tray drop-off point. They were testing him. Seeing if Darin would bow up, slink away, or pretend nothing was happening. He stepped to the side and offered for them to dump their trash and trays first. This forced the men to move along because of the pressure of the line behind them.

The largest of the men had a black beard and husky frame. He blew a kiss at Darin as he dumped and stacked his tray. The other two men laughed and encouraged each other in their fun. "First day at school," said one of the younger followers of Papa Bear.

Darin maintained a stoic countenance. He did not want them to have any emotional beachhead for their impending assault. There would be hell to pay. Darin could feel it. He had hoped for peace, but that was futile. Better to have open conflict than hidden pursuers. There was going to be no quarter given or received, and Darin accepted it. All his life, the hammer always fell as he felt it would. This will be no different, he thought.

Months went by. Papa Bear tried to groom him while they were together in their cell. At mealtimes, Darin would see the large men whisper and glance at him. One day to Darin's surprise the cook served him a berry pie. He was instantly flooded with the memory of his mother. Tears swelled in his eyes. With visible emotional vulnerability Darin walked past Papa Bear to his table. "I bet that pie is sweet" Papa Bear said to Darin with gnarled lust. Every day he was testing Darin and he wanted to be done with these men.

He tried to talk to the lead guard about what was happening. Darin quickly realized that the prison employees cared little about the sexual integrity of the inmates. Some even placed good money on what would happen to Darin and when.

One night, Darin woke up in his top bunk. It was the middle of the night, and the prison was quiet. He slipped off his bed and stood over Papa Bear as he watched the heavyset man labor to breathe. Darin plunged a shank made from a sharpened toothbrush into his neck. In a silent fury, Darin stabbed countless times until blood filled the air. The smell of iron and the bewildered flailing of the large man sent Darin into a berserk state.

Papa Bear was able to throw Darin off and get to his feet. He grabbed Darin by the neck and began strangling him. Darin could feel the blood squirting out of the man, but Darin continued to stab his neck in the fray. The two men fought for their lives in the dark. As Darin began to slip into unconsciousness, Papa Bear's grip loosened. His strength failed as his blood was lost.

Papa Bear died on top of Darin, and the two lay there like exhausted, drunk lovers. Darin didn't have the energy to lift the man off him. He was exhausted and could barely breathe. The incident was a small price to pay for freedom, though, as he gasped for air. Murmurings from the adjoining cells grew into loud shouts and a ruckus. The other inmates were intoxicated by the murder.

The prison lights went on. Litter flew from the cages of the excited men as they yelled and screamed. Darin could then distinguish the sound of guards stampeding down the corridor in full riot gear. He tried again to worm his way out from under Papa Bear's corpse. He had regained some strength because of the lights, the frenzied energy, and his own shock.

The guards were stacked at his cell gate. The lock clanged open, and they flooded in. They beat the limp bodies of Papa Bear and Darin with clubs like hunters from a prehistoric age. Darin took several blows to the head before the guards intuitively realized that the bulky man on top was dead. The energy changed, and the crazed beating turned into systematic control.

Papa Bear was lifted off while other guards restrained Darin by rolling him to his stomach and putting their full weight on him as he was zip tied. Some of the blood had already dried on Darin's hands and shirt. It was over. Papa Bear would never get to enjoy his lust, and Darin would be unmolested. What happened next mattered little to Darin.

As he was hauled out of his cell, the prison erupted in cheering. Many of the other men had been defiled by Papa Bear and his crew of sodomites. The guards marched Darin through a gauntlet of celebration. Darin was proud now; he had made the right decision. Never again would he be controlled, abused, and used by another.

Darin was restrained and questioned by the staff of the penitentiary. After he gave a full confession on the spot, he was placed in a holding cell alone. He knew that he would serve more time and would never see the world outside again. The price was worth it. It was better to rot in steel than be tormented by flesh. For the first time Darin could remember he slept and dreamed without terror.

Part 2

Above all, keep loving one another earnestly,
since love covers a multitude of sins.
1 Peter 4:8

Chapter 16

"Darin, come and eat; your food is getting cold," insisted his mother.

"I'm coming, Mom!" Darin cried as he bounded up the stairs.

The small table was set with mac n' cheese, hot dogs, and a glass of purple Kool-Aid. Darin's mother looked exhausted but happy, and Darin was hungry. The two sat themselves, and Darin's toes only grazed the floor. Darin's mom was no cook, but dinner was on time, and he never went hungry.

"Let's pray," said Susan as she clasped her hands and bowed her head.

Darin did the same as his mother and tried to stop his moving legs but found it difficult to stop altogether.

"Lord, thank you for this food, this home, and my son. May this meal nourish our bodies and minds, so that we can be of service to you and your kingdom. Amen," Susan said as she lifted her head and gave a faint smile to her son.

"Amen," he said with enthusiasm.

Darin grabbed his fork and started eating. Midway into his third or fourth sliced hot dog, Darin asked his mother for ketchup. With perceivable effort Darin's mother got to her feet, opened the fridge, and found Heinz. Noticing that the bottle was almost empty, Susan went to the sink and added a bit of water to the ketchup.

"Here you go, honey," Susan said as she poured some of the watery sauce on Darin's hot dog slices assembled in a partition of the plastic plate.

"Thanks, Mom," Darin said as he continued to master his utensil.

Mother and child sat alone eating dinner. A common thing; nothing great or unique but fundamental. There was a picture of Darin's father on the mantel by an encased folded flag. The location of the image made it so Darin's father was never out of sight when someone was in the living room or at the kitchen table.

William was younger when he and Susan met. They fell in love after high school, and Susan got pregnant. It was an unexpected consequence of young love, but the couple decided it was good and got married. William worked with his stepbrother Marty at landscaping and offered handyman services too.

The Vietnam war had been raging for a few years. Marty was unable to serve, and William wanted to join until he fell in love with Susan. Once she got pregnant, he decided that working with his stepbrother and providing for his new family would be his new priority. Men make decisions, but God directs their steps. William was drafted before his son was born, and he died in Vietnam as an infantry rifleman.

Susan had a baby boy and a flag to remind herself of his love.

The burden of loss made her sick. The doctors told her she had bone cancer when Darin was six years old. She never got over the loss of William. The pain of his death rotted her bones despite the gift of a son. Marty took over supplementing Susan's income. Darin thought of him as a father but knew that he was not his real papa. At every meal Susan would pray while looking at the portrait of her great man.

She drank occasionally to ease the pain caused by her cancer. She never got drunk in front of Darin, but she did struggle to maintain the house from time to time. She worked when she could with her sister, Donna, to help make ends meet. In this way the mother and child struggled on, making it day to day and meal to meal. Darin was surrounded by family and loss.

As Darin finished his dinner, Susan admired his likeness to William. "I have something for you," Darin's mother said as he ate his last bite of hot dog.

"What?" he said with excitement.

She revealed a berry pie still in the wrapper and opened it. She cut the frosted pie into two pieces and handed one half to him.

"Oh, thank you!" he exclaimed.

Susan smiled and nibbled on her piece, knowing that Darin would wolf his down and wait to see if his mother would eat all of her half.

The child and mother sat in the quiet evening in their modest home. After they finished the berry pie, Susan started to clean up the table and kitchen. Darin returned to his Star Wars battle scene. Luke Skywalker was being held captive by Darth Vader, and only the Force would save him.

"Time for a bath," Susan yelled from the kitchen.

"Ok, Mom!" Darin loudly responded, continuing his immersion in the great struggle between good and evil, light and dark.

"Darin!" Susan shouted.

"Coming," he said with realized urgency.

Darin's mom did not like to repeat herself this late in the day. He had learned to not push her patience after sunset. She was drained from the cancer by the end of the day, but Darin thought she was just tired.

The sea green tub filled quickly, and he tried to negotiate bringing his toys.

"Can I bring Yoda and Luke and the X-wing?"

"Not tonight, honey," his mother said softly.

Darin liked to recreate the scene where Yoda teaches Luke to lift the spacecraft out of the swamp. The bath was the perfect place to recreate their first attempt at mastering the Force.

"I must get to bed soon, Darin. No toys tonight," She said as she combed her hair.

Darin undressed and got in the tub. His mother always got the temperature right, and Darin never even considered that the water would be too hot or cold.

"Make sure to wash your whole body with soap," Susan said as she wiped makeup off her tired face.

"Ok, Mom, I will" he said as she left the bathroom.

Darin did as he was told, and when he was done, he tried to float in the tub. He liked to be as still as possible and rest on top of the water. His grandma had taught him to float in a lake before she died. He felt like every time he practiced, he could remember her. He had become pretty good at being buoyant and calm in the water.

"Time to get out," Susan said as she entered the bathroom with a towel and his one-piece pajamas.

As she draped the large threadbare towel around Darin, he shivered.

"Get dry, put on your pajamas, and then brush your teeth."

Darin nodded through clattering teeth.

He always thought his mother looked strange without make-up. As she was tucking him in, he studied her face. She seemed older; foreign but still maternal.

"Why don't you show me that you know your prayer, Darin." She said with a smile that can only come from love when a mother is as tired as she was.

"Ok, Mom," he exclaimed, excited to prove his ability with memory.

The child and mother held hands, and Darin searched his memory bank with squeezed eyes.

"Now I lay me down to sleep; I pray to the Lord my soul to keep; if I should die before I wake, I pray to the Lord my soul to take" Darin opened his eyes and scanned his mother's reaction to confirm that he had performed the prayer correctly. Her adoring gaze communicated that he had indeed finally memorized the prayer.

***

When Darin woke up, he was hungry. He never woke up without the need to eat something immediately. He scampered out of his bedroom and into the kitchen. He grabbed a box of cereal and made his way back to his room with the booty. His mother did not like it when he ate all the cereal without milk. She said it was a waste, but she was always asleep in the morning, and he did not know how to cook.

Fortified with snacks and a desire to continue the battle between Darth Vader and Luke Skywalker, hex left his mother alone. Darin played all morning in his pajamas. His room was bright, and if there was sunshine his room got its fill before any other room. The glow of sunlight and the immersion of imagination insulated Darin from the reality that his mother was sick.

Sometime in late morning or early afternoon, Darin heard his mother call out to him. Obediently he went to her room clutching the action figures. As he entered his mother's bedroom, the joy vanished, and the sun was barricaded by heavy curtains drawn. Darin felt for a moment he had used light speed to arrive on a dark planet.

"Call your aunt, Darin. Tell her to come here," Susan faintly said.

"What wrong, Momma?"

"I don't feel well again," his mother responded. "Get me a glass of water too when you come back."

Darin nodded his head and ran to the kitchen. He slid the kitchen table chair to the wall with the phone and looked at the number on the fridge. Lifting the receiver, he began cranking the rotary 5 ...0...3...,looking back at the number again...8...9...7. With anxiety Darin looked again at the number...3...3...6...9. With relief the phone made the ringing sound, and Darin waited.

"Hello!" said a loud and bullish woman's voice.

"Mom said to call you," Darin blurted.

"Oh, well what's going on?"

"Mom says she doesn't feel well and that I was supposed to call you."

"Is she able to come to the phone?" Donna asked

"No, she is in bed."

"I'll be right over, hon," Donna said with summoned femininity.

He hung up the phone, jumped off the chair and ran back to his mother to relay the information.

"Did you get me a glass of water?" Susan asked.

Darin felt shameful that he forgot, and his eyes started tearing up.

"I forgot."

Susan could hear the pain in Darin's voice.

"It's ok, darling. Just go get me some water, please," Susan stammered.

Darin ran back into the kitchen and pulled the chair from the wall by the phone and took it to the cabinet by the sink. He retrieved the glass and filled it to the brim. He then carefully lowered himself off the chair trying not to spill the water, but he did. He made his way to his mother's room with intense focus, but the water continued to splash out of the glass. With each step, Darin felt like he was failing his mother by losing water.

"I spilled some," Darin confessed.

Susan took the glass and grimaced as she tried to rouse herself.

"Hand me that orange bottle on the nightstand"

Darin did as he was asked and watched as his mother struggled to open it. Susan shook and trembled to master the childproof top on the bottle, and Darin could only watch. He had tried to open those bottles before but was never successful. Susan finally opened the pill container and poured out several little blue pills that looked like candy to Darin.

The pain was managed at the expense of alert consciousness. The little boy looked at his mother with confusion. She was not in pain, but she was unintelligible and vacant. Darin was glad that she took the pills, but every time she did, he felt alone and cold. The absence of a mother's full presence left a chill in the air. There is no greater feeling of emptiness for a child than that of being motherless.

The front door banged with undertones of aggression. Donna was here, Darin thought, as he rushed to the front door. Darin looked at her face through the glass as he unlocked the door. She looked angry but not at anything or anyone. Something in her burned that had no explanation. Darin both loved and feared his aunt.

Donna entered the house like she lived there. As she moved towards the bedroom, she looked at Darin and feigned a smile. Donna's expression felt like a fake gesture from a genuine source to him.

"Jimmy will be here soon so don't lock the door," Donna said.

"I won't," he said.

"Have you eaten?" Donna inquired, trying to alleviate at least a physical discomfort.

"I had some cereal," he answered quickly, fearing that he she would discover that he did not use milk.

"We'll get you sorted in a bit," she replied as she moved to her sister's bedroom with Darin in tow.

"Give me a moment alone with your mother," his aunt commanded.

Darin obeyed reluctantly. He retrieved his toys from his bedroom and began to play quietly. His imagination was stunted by feelings of guilt, but he went through the motions needing some sort of stimulation. This morning the dark side would gain the upper hand for Luke Skywalker was not ready to stand against the power of death. Darin could hear his aunt murmuring. What she was saying he could not understand, but he had never heard her be so quiet in all his life.

Another knock came to the door, and it was Jimmy. He was smiling and Darin liked him. He always made him laugh and would play with him like other adults rarely did. Clutching his action figures, Darin went to meet him as he entered the house.

"What's happening, my man?" Jimmy exclaimed.

"Mom isn't feeling very good again," Darin confessed.

"Yeah, Donna will get her sorted. How is the battle for the galaxy coming?" Jimmy asked, pointing to Darin's toys and changing subjects nimbly.

"Darth Vader is taking over, and the Jedi can't stop him anymore," answered the boy.

"Whoa, that's not right. The Jedi always overcome the Dark side!" Jimmy rebuked Darin with youthful enthusiasm.

"Well, I guess, but it doesn't always feel like it," his eyes were beginning to tear up.

"Come here, buddy," Jimmy sighed as he got to his knees and opened his arms.

He collapsed into Jimmy's embrace, and the flood of emotions began to pour out of him. Darin felt like he had to be strong until Jimmy arrived. Something about the man's presence faded the act, and he began to sob. He so wished that Jimmy was his father, but he was glad that he was here, even if his real dad could not be.

"Is Momma going to die?" Darin asked through gritted teeth

and a torrent of tears.

"I don't know, buddy. I wish I could tell you she won't die, but I don't know how long she has left," Jimmy said with a soothing tone while embracing his nephew.

The boy's agony increased, and Jimmy held on. The two stayed together until the boy became exhausted by the power of his emotions. When Jimmy stood up and went to the kitchen to make a cup of coffee, Darin went to the couch to lie down. Darin watched him as he looked for milk and sugar without finding them.

"Black coffee is an acquired taste, I suppose" said Jimmy as he came to sit with Darin.

"I think coffee is gross."

"Me too."

"Why do you drink it then?"

"Because I am old, and I do things I don't like to keep going," Jimmy answered, raising his cup and smirking.

Donna exited the bedroom. Her face was pale, and her bombastic manner was deflated. She shot a glance at Jimmy, and he understood immediately that Susan was not just temporarily sick.

"Darin, sweetie, will you give me and Uncle Jimmy a moment?" requested Donna.

"Up you get. Go and give Darth Vader the beating he deserves, heh? Galvanized by Jimmy's words, Darin rose and moved to his room, while Luke Skywalker began his comeback.

Chapter 17

Darin's new room was small but clean and warm. He missed his mother, but he was happy to have Jimmy. He had always wanted a father and a brother, and his uncle was both. Donna was strict, but Darin knew the rules and they were easy to follow. She ran the house, as she had always ruled her siblings. Her family let her be in charge, more out of love for Donna rather than acceptance of tyranny.

She was a loud, big woman who always knew what was needed to support her family. Even the men did as she bid without much resistance. Donna and Jimmy's home was larger than Darin's old house. His small room was in the basement, but it didn't feel like a subterranean subway. Jimmy, at Donna's command, had remodeled the unfinished basement to be fit for Darin. Jimmy installed carpet, drywall, and paint.

On Darin's wall was the picture of his father and a folded American flag in a shadow box. Next to his father was a picture of Darin's mother holding Darin beaming with maternal pride. Darin would look at these images often with love and with sadness. The wounds of children remain hidden to themselves despite the clarity of their damage to the adults if they pay attention.

Donna had a crucifix hanging in almost every room. Darin knew that the cross belonged to God and his son, but he did not know that he had a cross to bear himself. Donna made Darin keep his room clean, his nails cut, and his ears scrubbed. There was order, rarely at the cost of discipline, but never without the fear of it.

Donna had told Darin that he would be getting on with life and must get back to school and play with the other kids in the neighborhood. She said it was for his own good, and sometimes she would make him stay outside and play even if he did not want to. Luckily there was a park nearby that had swings and a large slide.

Darin would bring his toys to the park and play by himself as commanded. Darin felt alone even though Jimmy and Donna could see the park from the kitchen window. He did not like being forced to be outside and found it difficult to make friends. The other kids would tease him and bully him often.

The worst time came when a little girl and her brother took Luke Skywalker away from him. Darin would chase them and beg for his favorite toy's return, but the two little tyrants would throw Luke Skywalker back and forth out of Darin's reach and create agony for him.

The brother tossed the toy over Darin's head to the sister, who then ascended the tall slide ladder. As Darin began to climb after her, she held out the action figure and told Darin if he came any further, she would drop Luke and see if he could Skywalk. This made Darin stop. The line between imagination and reality was immediately suspended.

"Don't do it," Darin screamed.

"Then stay down there," commanded the little hobgoblin of a girl.

Darin began to cry and shake. He was overwhelmed with dread of his toy and hero being destroyed. Without thought, he picked up a rock and threw it at the little girl. The projectile hit her in the face, and she dropped the toy. And to everyone's shock, she plummeted and laid motionless on the hard ground. Darin approached the girl with terror. He saw blood oozing out of her head, and her eyes were closed.

"You killed her!" screamed the girl's brother.

The shock of seeing the little girl's body contorted and still with blood pooling around her head froze Darin. Her brother ran off screaming "She's dead, she's dead!" with his arms flailing. Darin moved closer and looked. Luke Skywalker was still in her hand. Darin bent down and retrieved his favorite action figure. Darin thought she was indeed dead but did not know what to do.

Darin stood over her, memorized and staring. Luke Skywalker became nothing more than a plastic mold. His hero, his idol, was no different than dead plastic. He hated the toy and threw it to the ground with disgust. Distant yelling broke the spell, and Darin looked to where the voice was originating. It was the girl's brother and a large man. The two were closing the distance, and fear compelled Darin to flee.

He ran into the house, and Donna and Jimmy were in the living room having a coffee.

"I killed her," Darin confessed.

The little boy was pale, slumped, and had completely resigned himself to the idea that she was dead.

"What are you talking about?" Donna said with immediate concern.

By instinct Jimmy got up and looked out the window and saw the man leaning over his daughter in the park.

"She's dead! I killed her with a rock!" Darin wailed as he ran off to his bedroom.

Donna looked out the window too and saw the commotion.

"Get out there and find out what is going on," said Donna to her husband.

Jimmy put his coffee down and did as he was commanded.

Donna went downstairs and found Darin with his head under his pillow. Darin felt like he was exploding, breaking. Something inside of him snapped, and he was beyond consoling. Repugnance, fear, guilt, regret, and shame mixed in the boy's body creating a storm of bewilderment and disconnect. The only clear thought that Darin had was that he had killed her. He could not be calmed. Donna just sat with him, keeping her hand on his back gently praying with a song-like tonality.

"Donna!" Jimmy said with urgency.

"Coming," Donna replied, understanding that she was needed immediately.

"Everything is going to be ok, buddy. I love you," Donna said to Darin as she patted his back once more and left him alone in his ocean of bewilderment.

Darin could hear adults arguing through the basement ceiling. The father is here, he thought to himself. He has come to get me. A second wave of dread flooded him. Darin roused himself despite the trembling and ascended the stairs to face the consequences of his actions. At the top of the stairs was a closed door leading to the living room. Darin paused behind the door. He could hear them talking and see the shadows of their movement.

"That little shit you've taken in damn near killed my daughter!" screamed the enraged father.

"Is she ok?" asked Donna, ignoring his volume and volatility.

"No, she is not ok. She might have a broken neck for all I know!" bellowed the large angry man.

"Oh, praise Jesus," Donna uttered with relief.

"Parise Jesus... did you hear me? She might have a broken neck!" snarled the man.

She is just relieved that your girl is alive, man" Jimmy inserted with summoned assertiveness.

Darin felt the agony begin to subside. Guilt and fear lessened but they still held dominion over his core.

"Listen, Bill. I'm sure it was an accident," Donna insisted.

"I want to see that punk right now," Bill hissed.

"Not a chance," answered Donna.

"Then all of you are going to answer to the cops," Bill threatened.

"I'd be happy to let you talk to Darin, but you have to calm down," Donna replied.

"Calm down?!" Bill screamed.

The man then grabbed the hands of his kids and bombarded down the stairs of the porch.

"We will be hearing from the police; I have no doubt," Donna said to Jimmy.

"What do you want to do?" asked Jimmy.

"We need to hear Darin's side of the story before they get here," Donna answered.

Darin opened the door and went upstairs into the living room. The boy's demeanor was deflated and sullen. He had heard that the girl was not dead, but a broken neck wasn't good. And he knew that could mean she could be paralyzed. Darin moved closer to Donna and Jimmy and allowed them to embrace him.

"What happened on the slide, Darin?" Donna inquired with newfound maternal frequency.

Darin explained the sequence of events and begged for forgiveness. He had no idea why he threw the rock; it just happened without thought. Donna and Jimmy listened and believed him.

"That Bill has always been a hothead. I am sure his daughter is going to be fine," Donna said while rubbing Darin's shoulder. Jimmy took a knee and hugged Darin.

"Don't worry, little buddy, this will blow over," Jimmy said, reinforcing Donna's comfort. Different tears expelled from Darin's eyes; tears of repentant sadness.

Later that evening a strong knock came on the door. The moment had arrived that Darin had been dreading. It was a police officer, and he looked serious. The porchlight cast shadows on the man's face, which exaggerated his features. He was wearing a patrol cap covered by transparent plastic. It had started raining as soon as Bill and his children left their house. Donna got up and answered the door.

"Hello, Officer," Donna said with ample humility.

"Good evening, ma'am. I'm Officer Caliban. Do you have time to answer some questions?"

"Absolutely, Officer. Please come in," Donna gestured as she spoke.

Officer Caliban removed his patrol hat and entered the house. He had an air of authority and seemed to be irritated.

"I suppose you know why I am here. I need to ask questions concerning the incident that happened at the park earlier today," Officer Caliban announced.

Jimmy and Darin watched on as Donna explained what transpired. The officer took notes and showed no emotion as he asked clarifying questions. The man in uniform gazed over at Darin, as Donna spoke, and Darin felt like his stare could detect lies. It made him uncomfortable because he knew he was guilty.

"Thank you, ma'am. Do you mind if I ask Darin some questions?" The officer requested.

"Actually, I do. He is just a boy, and it's been a long day," Donna said defiantly.

"That's fine, ma'am," replied Caliban with visible irritation.

"Tell that boy to keep his hands to himself and to keep away from the park," Officer Caliban said as he closed his notebook and started to exit the premises.

Donna followed the man out of the house. Darin could see her asking more questions of the officer. He was relieved that the policeman had left the house. He made Darin nervous, and the idea that he could arrest him was unsettling. Donna stood in a wide stance and crossed arms. She was not the type of person that could be easily intimidated. Darin loved her more than he ever had watching her defend him. What the exchange was about he could only guess. But he felt like she was trying to protect him from the policeman. The officer left, and Donna stood watching the patrol car exit the driveway with domineering authority. After the officer was gone, Donna looked up sensing Darin somehow and gave him a smile. Darin's relief was complete.

The bull of the woman ascended the stairs with a heavy but sturdy march. Darin and Jimmy were waiting expectantly as Donna entered. Both of them turned their attention towards their matriarch. Donna came in, walked back and forth in the kitchen a few times, searching for something but returning with a glass of water.

"What did he say, babe?" inquired Jimmy.

"Darin, why don't you go play downstairs for a bit?" Donna commanded gently.

"I want to know what he said too," Darin said imploringly.

"It was nothing bad, but us adults need to talk, and I think you could use a break too," Donna answered in a rare explanation to having a demand questioned.

Darin accepted her answer and rushed to Donna and gave her a hug. His eyes started to tear up again, and he squeezed her tightly.

"I did not mean to hurt that girl," Darin murmured through fresh tears.

"There, there, I know. Now go play and try to calm down," Donna said.

Darin let go of Donna, gave Jimmy a quick hug, and retreated to the basement.

Chapter 18

The rock incident kept the cobbled family in court for the rest of the year. Their insurance was billed to pay for the medical care of the little girl. She had suffered a concussion and a sprained neck. In the legal process, the state thought it best that Darin receive mental health counseling. He was appointed a provider and had to attend several sessions.

Darin thought of himself differently now. He feared his anger and his unpredictable behavior. He could kill someone, and this realization robbed him of innocence. He played differently and alone, always wary of bullies and his own temper. His dad was a soldier, so maybe he had inherited something from him that needed to be contained and controlled.

Darin was brought to a drab building with several offices. Donna and Darin found the location of his new counselor, Dr. Jessica Dodd. She was on the second floor, Room 2C. The pair searched for the elevator and ended up taking the stairs. Donna said they would find the lift on their next visit when they had more time. Darin felt lost in this building; everything was brown and uniform.

Dr. Dodd's office door had an engraved name tag on the solid wood door just like all the other offices in the building. The apprehension that filled the boy was great. What if she thought he was crazy or evil? Would she be able to help him? What was wrong with him anyway? Donna knocked on the door, but no one answered. She looked at her watch and saw that it was two o'clock. Not wanting to be late Donna decided to enter.

As the door opened, Donna was relieved to see that the first door was to a waiting room. No longer feeling like she was late, the pair sat down and tried to ignore the voices coming from the therapist's proper office. Donna leaned close to Darin and whispered: "You are not crazy. You just have to talk to this person because the state wants to make an effort to help troubled kids."

Darin nodded and picked up a magazine displayed on the coffee table. He picked one that seemed the least adult and thumbed through it like a respectable person would as they waited. Donna bounced her right leg in a fast and rhythmic manner. The room smelled of industrial cleaning products and stale paper. On the wall was a picture of Mt. Hood, and a lavender field. Both pictures seemed fake to Darin.

He had never seen Mt. Hood look like it did in this picture. Darin wondered if other people saw places like they were depicted in these photos. Why didn't he see it like they did?

"Aunt Donna, why does Mt. Hood look like that?" Darin blurted while pointing to the picture.

"Shush," Donna said with an air of irritation. "Don't be so loud. There is someone in that office, and we don't want to disturb them," Donna explained after she composed her initial reaction that visibly upset Darin.

"The photo is overedited. They do that to make photos look more interesting," Donna explained in a whisper.

"But it looks fake," Darin argued.

"Yes, it does, but people like that sometimes," Donna continued.

"Why don't people like things the way they really are?" Darin asked.

"Because some people have the time and money to make things seem better or stranger than they really are to make their lives more interesting," Donna said with a smirk.

"What about those rows of flowers?" Darin asked.

"The lavender fields sometimes do look that purple at sunset," Donna explained, taking a moment to appreciate the image.

The office door opened, and two women emerged. One was an older woman with grey hair that seemed perfectly managed, and the other was younger wearing strange clothes Darin had never seen before. The older woman had been crying but Darin could see that they were tears of relief. Jimmy had always told him that "Only the eyes of women get wet!" Darin didn't believe him, but he got the message. Men don't cry, especially in public. The woman in the baggy and colorful clothes patted the older woman on the back and rubbed a little between each pat.

"It's going to all work out in the end," Dr. Jessica Dodd affirmed with a tilted head and empathetic eyes.

The older woman began to weep a little more as she brought the wet tissue to her eyes to absorb the tears before any more mascara could run. It was strange to see a person freely release emotions while maintaining a sense of vain composure. Darin liked women but found them to be contradictory and disarming. The two women embraced, and the counselor seemed to genuinely send comfort through her body to the elderly woman.

Darin decided that he will not be hugging this woman, nor crying, as he waited to be introduced and sent into a room where this woman might make him cry about things he didn't want to cry about anymore. After all, wasn't that the point? She couldn't bring back her mother or father. She couldn't heal the little girl's neck. Darin didn't like the state of Oregon, Dr. Dodd, or offices with edited pictures.

He wanted to be home with Jimmy or playing with his toys in the park; well, the park without bratty kids that fall too easily. The counselor kept her attention on the old woman until she had left the office. Then she turned to Donna and Darin, smiled warmly at Darin, said hello, and then addressed Donna with a warm greeting. Dr. Dodd presented her hand to Donna for a handshake, and when Donna gave her hand, the doctor gently clasped Donna's hand with both of hers. Something about that bothered Darin; it felt too nice, too warm like people being kind in church but changing as soon as the pastor excused them. Bill, the girl's father, was like that. He would be sentimental and ingratiating during Sunday service. Then later that Sunday he yelled at his kids and wife like he never stepped in God's house, not even once.

Dr. Dodd then acknowledged Darin by bending over to be on eye level with him. This made Darin uncomfortable. The counselor noticed, and after she made her practiced introduction, she stood erect and disengaged from her theatrical empathy.

"Well, should we get started?" Dr. Dodd inquired, looking

for consent from Donna and agreement from Darin.

"That sounds good to me. What time should I return?" Donna asked.

"The first session runs a little over an hour, but after we establish rapport, the sessions usually conclude on the hour," Dr. Dodd replied.

"I'll be back in an hour and a half then?" Donna asked.

"That will be fine," responded the therapist. "Then we are agreed," Dr. Dodd declared with an inviting smile to Darin.

Darin followed her gesture to enter the room where the counseling would take place. He felt like he was walking on to the Death Star. In the room Darin noticed some pictures, but there were not any kids. There were strange masks on the walls, all of them were foreign and intimidating to Darin.

"The masks are to remind us that we all wear a face at times different than who we really are," expressed Dr. Dodd as she entered the room, noticing Darin's curiosity.

There were two chairs facing each other but at an angle. The councilor extended her hand to the chair on Darin's right side. He took his seat as did the therapist. The two sat in silence for a moment that seemed like a long time to Darin. He avoided eye contact, but the silence forced him to look at her. Dodd's eyes lit up, and she smiled again.

"How are you doing today on a scale of one to ten, ten being the best you've ever felt, one being the worst?" The mind wizard asked.

Darin paused for a moment calculating his answer.

"There are no wrong answers. We will do this every session to establish what I like to call a baseline," Dr. Dodd said.

"I'm about seven," Darin blurted.

Darin felt that a "seven" would be a reasonable answer and a safe one. As soon as he gave his number, Dr. Dodd smiled like she knew that it was a lie. "That's good," replied Dodd. "Today is mostly about paperwork and familiarity. Let's get the formality out of the way, shall we?" Dr. Dodd asked.

Darin agreed, and Dr. Dodd ran through a series of questions and statements that Darin found boring and confusing. The counselor explained that if he told her that he was going to hurt himself or another person that she would have to report to the police. She also informed Darin that if she discovered that someone was hurting him, she would have to report that too.

She asked Darin if he understood why they were meeting and what their responsibilities were. Every time she stated something, she compelled Darin to answer that he understood. He did not understand, but he wanted to seem like an intelligent guy that knew what he was doing. After a litany of rules, explanations and formalities, the two sat in silence some more.

"Why do you think we are here Darin?" Dr. Dodd asked Darin.

"Well, Doctor..."

"Call me Jessica please, Darin," The therapist interrupted.

"Oh, sorry. I will do that," Darin said with a mix of feelings.

"Sorry to interrupt. Again, why do you think we are here today?"

"Because I hurt that girl on the slide," Darin said with shame.

"Yes, that is part of it but what else?"

"I don't know," said Darin.

Jessica paused and repositioned herself ever so slightly. Darin searched his conscience and memory. Had he hurt someone else? Did this doctor know something he had forgotten? Darin sat in silence too and waited for her to tell him, since he had no idea. Jessica let the silence linger, but she could see that Darin did not have another answer.

"Darin, how have you been feeling since your mother died on a scale of one to ten?" Jessica looked relieved to address the painful fact that compelled the State of Oregon to intercede by enrolling Darin in a new program.

"I feel like a zero," Darin responded with his head hung low and tears forming.

Donna was on time to pick Darin up. Leaving Darin with a stranger that was going to help him filled her with jealousy and confidence. Jessica and Donna engaged in a quick brief about the next steps and then she and Darin made their way out of the building. The therapist ended the session shortly after Darin's confession of pain due to the death of his mother. She had told him that they needed to work through the pain. Jessica used the analogy of laying around after getting physically hurt.

Jessica had told him, "When I was young, I broke my back. The physical therapy hurt so much. But the doctors told me that if I did not do the exercises, I would always struggle to walk." She continued by connecting her story to his. "Darin, if you do not work through your emotional pain now, it could become much harder to do so in the future." Darin did not want to think about his mother because then he would think about his dead father too. One thought would lead to another, and he would feel lost and alone.

Donna gave Darin concerned glances at stoplights. Darin could feel her desire to help him and tend to his wound. All she could do was feel for him. She did not know what to do or say. Most of her life had been about fixing other people's problems. Over the years she had come to realize that she had a hard time watching people suffer, especially her family. She had become a fixer, more to make herself feel better than the person she was trying to help.

Donna was committed to being a rock for Darin. She fought off the urge to get him ice cream or buy him toys on the ride home. She knew that he needed to process the session. Dr. Dodd explicitly requested that she not do such a thing until a later time. So, the woman and the boy sat in still silence inside of the moving noise. Driving was like that; alone but in public, separate but moving in unison, alone but together.

When they pulled in the driveway, Donna turned off the car and took a big breath.

"Are you hungry?" she asked.

"A little," Darin answered.

Donna's eyes were watering, and Darin felt uncomfortable because his tears were absent. He wanted to cry but couldn't. He always seemed to cry when others were happy and laugh when others were sad. Darin didn't know why, but other people's emotions made him rebellious and distant.

"It's okay, Aunt Donna," Darin said, while glancing at her.

"Okay," Donna said self-consciously, reaching for and patting Darin's shoulder.

The duo exited the car and made their way up the stairs to the second floor living room. To Darin's relief, Jimmy was home and in good spirits. He was a simple man, lighthearted, fair, and funny. Darin trusted him and could be himself around Jimmy.

"What's up, my man?" Jimmy said with a beaming smile as he rose from the couch.

"Not much."

"Did you get your head checked out?"

"Yeah...I did," answered Darin shyly, smiling.

"Good; got to keep the nuts and bolts tight," Jimmy said with animation.

Jimmy scuffed Darin's hair and hugged Donna. Jimmy's easy-going nature and jokes edged on Donna, but she contained herself seeing that Darin liked the jests.

"Are we going to eat?" Jimmy announced and inquired.

"The groceries are in the car," she said.

"Yes, Ma'am! C'mon, Darin. Help me get the chow out of the car," beckoned Jimmy as he made his way out the door. Darin followed, happy to be employed and freed of emotional confinement.

Dusk was settling in; the air was crisp, and his heart felt a little lighter while carrying heavy bags. Donna was in the kitchen with her apron on preparing to cook. Jimmy and Darin laughed and were glad. Donna only wore her apron when she was baking a cake or making pizza.

Chapter 19

Darin had turned into a strong young man, withdrawn but agreeable. He liked to work with Marty, a cousin of Donna and his mother. Life had not been easy on Marty. His wife left him, and he had bouts where he struggled with the drink. Marty was always sober on the job and had been working though the Alcoholics Anonymous twelve steps. Marty called it AA and made it a point to hit a meeting every day.

Sometimes Darin would have to go along with Marty to these meetings. The AA visits excited Darin, but he disliked the smoke-filled rooms. Marty smoked more in the meetings. He said the other drunks "made him do it because if he was going to smell it, he might as well smoke himself." The duo would usually arrive just in time for the meeting and seat themselves in any open spot.

It was hard to imagine the Holy Spirit hanging out in the smoke-filled den of these oddballs. But Darin could feel God's presence more in AA than he ever did during church on Sunday. There was something about these people that Darin could sense God loved. He was almost jealous that he was not an alcoholic. The desperate disposition of these men and women seemed to give greater access to humility and spiritual clarity.

Marty's personality flourished inside these buildings. He became more generous and funnier. Darin rarely saw the humorous and lighthearted side of Marty outside of AA participation. Most of the time Marty would hit a meeting after dropping Darin off at the end of the workday. However, the current job in Lake Oswego was "testing me," Marty would say. Around noon Marty would beckon Darin to tidy up and go to a meeting with him.

Of all the damage done by Marty and his drinking, it was his truck that bore the brunt of the chaos. The old white vehicle had been through hell and back but kept on rolling, to Marty's amazement. "This damn truck was made for times like these," he would say every time it started after a series of pumps and cranks that only a long-time owner could master.

Today was one of those days, and Marty came up to Darin as he was pulling up old fence posts. "Has the owner been flaunting herself by the window again? Marty asked, already knowing the answer.

"She sure has," replied Darin.

"She is good looking, but something is wrong with her," Marty said, while scanning quickly to detect Melissa's presence.

The two laughed, and Marty gestured for Darin to come along. Darin set his tools down and followed Marty to the truck. A drizzle that had been threatening rain began as the men got into the crusty, but dry, truck. Marty performed the ritual, and the old workhorse started. Marty, clearly pleased with himself, patted the dash and gave Darin a wide grin.

"Ain't nothing wrong with this truck that understanding and

patience can't overcome," Marty said partly to Darin, himself, and to his vehicle.

Darin was glad that they were out of the rain. He felt fresh and clean until Marty lit a cigarette. He did not say anything. He knew Marty was addicted and self-conscious of his lingering habit.

"It's funny you know; I can plug the jug but can't seem to kick the smoke," Marty said, sensing Darin's repulsion to the smell. They both cracked their windows open and pulled out of the driveway.

"Don't look; there she is, watching us," Marty said, taking a drag as he observed into the rearview mirror. "What a strange damn woman," Marty concluded as he turned his attention to the road at the end of the drive.

Darin sneaked a peak in his mirror and could see the owner in her doorway with a posture of disappointment and air of sexual presence. He wondered why she was the way she was. Did something happen to her? Was she always like this? Melissa would saunter around any window that the men were working by. If you looked, she would become incensed if you did not look her gestures, and movement would increase until it was awkward enough that a body would have to take notice. Then she would act offended and leave the room.

So that's how the job went. Marty and Darin would keep their heads down and avoid her leers only to agitate the woman more. Then they would shuttle off for breaks to gird themselves for the last half of the workday. It was a game of cat and mouse that neither wanted to play but was forced to endure because the job paid well, and Marty needed income.

Marty knew the Portland area like the back of his hand. He

made it to Oregon City from Lake Oswego in no time while taking all
the short cuts that only a native that was used to avoiding authority
could master. The habit of taking side routes through neighborhoods
was a vestige of his drinking days. His license was renewed, he was
sober, and the truck was legal, yet he slinked and dashed as if he was
being pursued.

Marty got to the old church building right at noon, crushed
out his cigarette, and the two exited the truck.

"Lock your door, Darin. These drunks may help keep me sober, but they still steal my shit!" Marty said with seriousness.

Darin did as he was told and wondered how was it that a person would go to a meeting about truth, humility, and willingness, yet
still pilfer his fellows?

Such is the way of men, thought Darin. Beg for mercy, steal
their bread, and then confess when the bread ran out. He did not feel
superior to these drunks. He felt like one of them. Abandoned, misunderstood, agitated by an invisible need that never is satisfied. Always
searching but never finding. Darin was glad that the alcoholics had
found a way to live. Deep down he hoped that some of their peace
would spill over to him. Darin even thought about becoming a drunk
so that he could fully partake in AA as a member and not as a visitor.

Darin followed Marty through the doors of the church. They
walked down the hall and could hear and feel the warmth and hear the
joy emanating from the room where the meeting was being held. As
they entered the meeting area, some of the men turned their heads to
see who was approaching, recognizing Marty and Darin with warm
smiles and even perceivable joy at their arrival.

Marty and Darin took their seats next to an old-timer, and

the meeting began. There was comfort in the certainty of the AA process that Darin appreciated. The members took turns going though preliminaries that every meeting started with. One man read the Promises, another the twelve steps, and yet another the twelve traditions. Darin settled in and let the magic or God of these men comfort and calm him.

George, an old man who still retained an air of power from his days as an Airborne Ranger, got up to speak. "I was and still am a dirty rotten son of a bitch. Without God, I would just as soon spit on a man or shoot him down. When I was young my father died, and my mother married a fella that worked at the machine shop in Portland. Every night he would come home, and he would beat the tar out of me and my mother.

"I hated that man, if you can call him that. We lived in a hovel full of terror and cold. Bill was a big man, a sour man; never once did he offer me a word of kindness or love. One night he came home late, and my mother and I knew that meant trouble. My mother, God rest her soul, explained to me that I should go to my room and stay in it no matter what I heard. I agreed and went into my room with my pajamas on and committed to honor my mother's request.

In fear I laid in my bed, if you can call it that; more of a pallet, really. I laid in my bed and tried to push out the anxious thoughts with no success. I don't remember when he came home, whether I was still awake or was awakened. But what followed was the worst night of my life before or after the war. I heard the door open, then silence. I heard some muffles and a thud. Frozen in fear I waited, and to my relief that was the end of it. I remember being buzzed with comfort, and I went to sleep.

"When I woke up for school the next day Bill was gone, and my mother lay stone-cold dead on the floor. The man, my stepfather, had strangled her. Apparently, Bill had heard some comments that his wife was too pretty for him and was a cheater. It did not matter that my mother was terrified of the man and feared God too much to be an adulteress. Old Bill's insecurities and jealousy did not need evidence to be possessed with rage."

Darin was floored by the vividness and bluntness of this old man's story. He was always ashamed that he did not have a father, and he was angry that his mother died. His mother never remarried, and Darin was grateful that he did not have an evil stepfather but still longed for a dad. Marty and Jimmy had tried to fill the void, but he still felt the hole in his life, despite their efforts to be placeholders.

The old man continued, "I swore to my Maker that I would never again be at the mercy of any man. I ended up in an orphanage. Some of those kids got molested, and some of them did not. It was the kind and scared kids that got taken advantage of. I entered that sordid place determined to kill any son of a bitch that laid a hand on me. I did not get buggered, but I had my share of violence. As soon as I turned eighteen, I enlisted in the Army and found myself in the Korean war.

"I was an alcoholic before I ever took a drink. The first dram of booze I took a swig of confirmed it. I went through the war killing any damn thing that moved and drinking any liquid that had alcohol in it. I was a terror of a man, but never a coward, never afraid of death. I was, and still am, afraid of life. My wife left me, my children want nothing to do with me, and I am now an old man full of sad stories with a house devoid of laughter.

"God relieved me of the craving ten years ago. I am grateful for my freedom from the drink, but I still feel empty and alone. The men in this room are my father, my children, and my life." The other men in the room sat in silence. Some had heard this story before, but many had not. Darin felt an enormous wave of guilt and gratitude wash over him. He had Jimmy, Marty, and Donna. He had family. He missed his mother and longed for a father, but life can be cruel, and love dies.

"I have learned that there is evil in this world, but we can resist it if we look to God. I waited too long to redeem my physical life, but God is never late, and my last days on this earth are being filled with the Promises in this book." The old man enveloped by the power of truth held the Big Book in his hand. "I will die and my story with me, but you men still hanging on to "Old Ideas" need to learn from my story."

Darin's eyes began to fill with tears. He was convinced to allow his extended family to love him. He would forgive his mother and father for abandoning him even though they did nothing wrong except die. Darin could not remember what else the old man said. His thoughts and feelings were turned inward for the rest of the meeting. Marty got up and said a few words, but then remained distant as the echo of the old man's warning loomed forefront in Darin's thoughts.

The meeting was concluded, and the men shook hands and hugged. Darin thought about approaching the veteran but decided there was no point. He had nothing to say or ask that hadn't already been said or thought. Marty was his usual self. Darin heard him laughing and jesting. Marty thrived on the fellowship, and he always made his rounds to greet or joke with the men at the end of meetings. Darin decided right there that he would never touch alcohol. He had a sense that whatever lurked in that old man was present in himself.

With no one left to banter with, Marty was ready to leave the church and go back to the jobsite. The two men got unlocked and started the truck. Marty lit a cigarette and took a big breath.

"I love those meetings," Marty said as he exhaled a plume of smoke.

Darin remained silent, contemplating the menacing feelings that he could feel but not name.

"Hey, bud, you doing alright? Ready to get back to work?" Marty said, dimly aware that Darin was withdrawn.

Darin forced a smile and acknowledged Marty with a nod. Marty made his way back to the job, this time taking the main roads while maintaining a speed that was consistent and calm. As they pulled into the driveway, Darin spotted a shadow retreat from the window of the homeowner. There was something wrong with Melissa, but instead of feeling intrigued or put off by her strange mannerisms, Darin realized that there might be something wrong with everyone, including himself.

Darin returned to the old fence post he was extracting and kept digging. He could feel the dark-haired woman leering at him. She wanted to be noticed but feared herself at the same time. Just like Darin longed for love but couldn't bring himself to express it. Darin prayed for the woman. He had been told over and over in church to pray for others, but never did. For the first time in his life, he saw the situation for what it was. This beautiful, but threatening, woman was this way despite Darin and Marty. There was nothing wrong with them. She was just playing out her own dramas.

Marty didn't rip people off, and Darin did not undress women with his eyes. Other men had done that to Melissa, and now Marty and Darin were paying for it. There was no purpose in admiring her or in detesting her. The only recourse was to pray for her and hope that God would give her comfort in His way and in His time if she was willing to receive it. Her shadows grew fainter, and Darin's sadness abated. The work for the day was done, and the two men finished their labor with satisfaction.

Chapter 20

Darin woke up on Tuesday morning grateful that Marty had given him time off. He felt lighter and more connected to himself and God. He made his way up the stairs to the kitchen early, unable to sleep in because he had been conditioned by his work schedule. Donna was preparing food, and Darin was a little annoyed. He was looking forward to a coffee in silence.

"Good morning," Darin announced before approaching Donna.

"Jesus!" cried Donna.

"I'm sorry, I thought it would be better to say something rather than just walk up on you. I know you do not like being surprised," Darin said as he went for the coffee pot, happy that at least he did not have to make it.

"It's fine, why don't you make some sounds when you're moving about? You're like a cat, I never hear you coming," Donna joked with some seriousness.

Darin stomped his feet in an exaggerated manner with a grin.

"Knock it off, you'll wake up Jimmy, and then I won't get

anything done," Donna whispered loudly.

"Sorry," Darin said as he found his favorite large coffee cup.

Darin poured himself the coffee and was pleased that he did not take the last of it. That would require him to make a fresh pot, which he did not want to do now that he had the stimulant in hand, ready for consumption. The first time Marty offered Darin coffee on a jobsite, Darin asked where the cream and sugar was. Marty had told Darin that "men drink coffee black as tar." From then on, Darin abstained from cream and sugar even though he missed them. Strong black coffee was beginning to taste as good as it made him feel.

Darin took his coffee to the couch and sat looking out the window at the morning sun chasing off the fog and dew. His muscles were sore, and his body felt fatigued, but feeling physically worn down only heightened his feeling of satisfaction. Holidays were enjoyable if he felt like he earned them. Warm is sweeter after being cold; food tastes better after getting very hungry; and rest feels better after exertion.

Donna moved with a sense of urgency as she always did. If Donna was awake, there would be organizing, laboring, and scuttling to and fro. Darin wondered if she enjoyed her relentless toil or if she needed it. Perhaps her thoughts vexed her when she was still, or maybe her internal source of energy prodded her on simply because she had more life force than others.

"What's going on today?" Darin asked more out of politeness than curiosity.

"Miranda and her daughter are coming over for a bit this morning," Donna answered, staying focused on her work.

Donna's answer took a moment to penetrate Darin's sleepy

mind. Miranda's daughter... Shannon!

"You mean Shannon?" Darin asked, trying to conceal his earnest interest.

"She has only one daughter, Darin," Donna said, oddly annoyed.

"What time are they coming over?" Darin asked.

"Around ten, now let me be," Donna said with finality.

Donna never liked to talk when she worked, and she disliked resting people in her presence if she was engaged in cleaning or cooking. Darin paid closer attention and realized that Donna was cleaning the kitchen and prepping brunch. Donna had met Miranda at a church function. They were involved in a women's Bible study. There were supposed to be two other women, but they dropped out once they realized that Bible studies involved studying. Just Donna and Miranda remained, and they were taking turns hosting.

Shannon was beautiful. Darin was enticed and drawn to her from the first time he met her. She was going through a divorce, and Darin felt like her husband, or soon to be ex-husband, was abusive. Shannon had a glow that she concealed. She was elegant and flirtatious by nature. Years of verbal degrading had dimmed her true colors, but light cannot be totally consumed. The few times that Shannon had tagged along with her mother to his house had been enthralling.

Darin will never forget the first time he met her. He was still in sweats and hadn't showered yet. Donna had already made light sandwiches and was setting the table when the two women knocked on the door. Darin was uninterested in church ladies coming over. He had thought to himself that he would hang out in the living room until they showed up. When they did arrive, he would say hello and retire to the basement room to enjoy his Saturday in quiet.

They knocked on the door and Donna opened it. Miranda was attractive for an older lady, and Darin was surprised. Then straggling behind was Shannon. Tall, aware, and holding presence. Darin immediately became acutely aware of the dirt under his fingernails, his uncombed hair, and the stains on his joggers. She looked at him bemused, sensing his insecurities, and said hello with an extended hand. Darin approached her as if naked, shook it, smiled, and then retreated to the basement.

That would not happen today. Darin rushed to his shower, cleaned himself in record time, put on slacks and a clean shirt, and reappeared upstairs. Donna glanced out the corner of her eye and then turned to face Darin squarely. She seemed unimpressed when her countenance changed.

"Shannon is beautiful, no?" Donna asked with flatness.

Darin, blushing at such directness, nodded his head in affirmation. The very mention sent awkwardness through his being, and Darin's face reddened at his inability to conceal his attraction to Shannon.

"You know she is still married, right?" Donna stated more than asked, but a response was expected.

"I thought she was getting a divorce," Darin said in a slightly defiant manner.

"She is separated, but the church is trying to help them reconcile. You best mind yourself and not interfere between a man and his wife," Donna scolded with warm eyes that communicated sensitivity.

"I just want to say hello, is that all right with you?" Darin asked, regaining his composure.

"Fine, then help me set the table, say your peace, then leave us to our Bible study," Donna said as she continued her work.

Darin got a rag and the cleaning spray and started wiping down the table. As he began cleaning, the entire house seemed to come alive with dust and debris. Just moments ago, the house seemed clean and warm with the morning sun. Now that very same light highlighted every blemish that might reveal their uncleanliness. Darin started to sweat through his fresh shirt, but he continued to clean and organize.

Just as the table was set and the upper floor was cleaned as best that Darin could do on short notice, the two women arrived and knocked. Donna removed her apron and donned a genuine smile. She opened the door and invited the mother and daughter to enter. The fresh air of morning, combined with the scent of Shannon, floored Darin. He stood frozen with a spray bottle in one hand and a rag in the other, with visible underarm sweat.

"Say hello, Darin," Donna said, trying to cue her adopted son and save him from embarrassment.

Darin flushed at the focus brought on him and eked out a greeting. Donna asked to take their coats, and the women sat themselves at the kitchen table. Shannon had cut her hair, a sign to Darin that the divorce was as good as done. She seemed more confident, like a wealthy person that had lost their fortune but no longer needed to struggle to hang on to appearances and was free to start over. Darin knew that she would be his and, in some way, Shannon confirmed his passion by an invisible signal that only future lovers can understand.

"Can I get you a coffee?" Darin asked Shannon.

"Oh yes, please," Shannon responded with large eyes that could disarm a hungry lion.

Darin moved to the coffee pot and saw to his horror that Donna had taken the last cup, breaking her own rule of making a fresh brew.

"You will have to start a new pot," Donna said, unaware of the internal pressure Darin was enduring.

"Okay," Darin responded with mild frustration.

Should he make it strong or light? All they had was Folgers. If Darin would have known Shannon was coming, he would have gone downtown and found some coffee with a name like Breakfast Delight, or Morning Thunderstorm, made by people that wore black and understood acidity, body, and roasting methodology. He would have got anything but Folgers. Waiting for the new pot to fill was a form of torture. Darin felt extreme anxiety over the drip and had to resist the urge to pull the filling pot and give her a cup. He knew that when coffee was rushed it was too bitter for anyone unless they were addicted to caffeine.

The brew was finished. Darin found a clean mug, poured the coffee into it, and then walked over to Shannon carefully because he had overfilled it. Darin sat the mug down and was rewarded by a smile, an invitation, a recognition of his admiration for the young woman.

"Thank you, Darin. You wouldn't happen to have any cream and sugar, would you?"

Darin smiled at Shannon and then turned to Donna, who was engaged in small talk with Miranda. Realizing that Donna's starvation for the female community was being satiated, Darin turned back and looked at Shannon.

"I'll check. I'm sure we have sugar, but we might not have cream," Darin said like a confession.

"Milk would be fine too," Shannon said, putting Darin at ease.

Darin hopped to and opened the fridge, and to his great relief there was a gallon of milk. He grabbed the jug, shut the door, and headed back to the table. As if by instinct, Donna got up and intercepted Darin. She grabbed his arm and redirected him to the cabinet and showed him the ceramic sugar and creamer set.

"But the milk and sugar hit these," Donna said, before grabbing some paper towels for napkins.

Darin loved Donna more than before that day. She was paying attention, and she did not let her nephew embarrass himself. Darin made his way back to the table with the proper presentation and was calmed.

"Thank you," said Shannon as she looked Darin directly in the eyes.

Darin absorbed her glow, facial proportions, and warmth, like a starving man would embrace a bowl of hot soup. Darin loved her and she knew it.

"Alright Darin, let us ladies talk awhile," Donna interrupted.

Shaken from his enthrallment, Darin acknowledged his aunt and made his way from the table. Before he reached the door to the basement, he asked if he could be notified before they left so he could say good-bye. Donna agreed, and Darin exited reluctantly, yet inspired. Darin had noticed many beautiful women before, but none had noticed him, and he loved Shannon all the more for it.

Darin laid in his bed, forlorn. He yearned for Shannon, with lust, passion, and even agony. He knew to even desire a woman that was married was adultery. God's word and Darin's desire went to war in his body and mind. The three women above had no idea that mortal conflict was taking place beneath their feet. Darin's will would pose questions to God, and, in some undefinable way, God's spirit answered. Was it really a sin to desire a beautiful woman? Without sound and from within himself, yet originating from some other source knowing that the answer was "yes," took hold. What do I do then? Pray for her and her husband. Pray?! Yes.

Darin felt his lust transmute into compassion. He stopped seeing Shannon as erotic and alluring. Instead, he started seeing her as stuck, besieged by the greyness of faithfulness and ignorance of the sanctity of the marriage vow. Had not her husband defied that vow to love Shannon by hitting her and belittling her? Why did the church continue to compel this fair woman to fulfill her husband's vow alone. Darin had heard that Shannon and her mother went to the church elders to obtain a blessing from them to leave her husband. To Shannon and Miranda's shock, they declared that would be a sin and that the two women should be praying for him instead of separating a family.

As Darin wrestled with morality, his room started to feel small and boyish. A real man would have his own house, his own cream and sugar to serve in the appropriate vessels, he thought. Darin turned his inquisition on himself and remembered that God said that a man would leave his family and make his own. In that moment, Darin decided that he would stop being agreeable with Donna and get his own place. Donna told him that while he was working it made more sense for Darin to stay with her and Jimmy.

Rent was expensive, and it did little good to pay bills alone. At first this made sense to Darin. Donna and Jimmy treated him fairly and he did contribute. However, as this moment was proving, he did not have an equal say, and when Donna said go, he went. Darin decided that starting on Monday he would begin the search for a place of his own.

Minutes felt like hours, yet hours went by in what felt like minutes, and Darin heard and felt the commotion of people getting ready to leave. Irritated that Donna had not summoned him to say good-bye, Darin roused himself out of bed, straightened his shirt, and made his way up the stairs. As he opened the door, something blocked it. Darin peered around the door, instead of forcing it, and saw Donna.

She smiled and stepped aside. Ashamed of his quickness to vilify his aunt, Darin entered the room with sudden humility.

"Miranda and Shannon are getting ready to leave," Donna said with a small smile.

Darin nodded his head and made his way to Shannon.

"It was good to see you. Will you be at church Wednesday?" he asked, completely aware of his rigidness.

Shannon, blushing slightly, glanced at her mother for support or permission. She then turned to Darin and said that she and her husband would be attending. Darin flattened like a tire that had just run over a nail. But not all was lost. He could sense that there was more regret than formality in Shannon's response.

"What a great brunch, Donna," Miranda blurted as she gently gripped Shannon's arm about her elbow.

"It was nice to talk with you, Darin," Miranda said more as an employed royal attendant than a mom who just ate at his house.

Darin realized that the group of women were shutting him down, and that any more effort from him would worsen his cause rather than assist it.

"It was great to see you both today. Please drive home safely," Darin expressed with a straight back and featureless face.

As soon as the words left his lips, he regretted his default setting of stonewalling due to any perceived rejection. The three women repeated their good-byes, as women do, and Darin stood sentry over his own embarrassment. Motionless he watched as Shannon left, helpless yet resisting the urge to blurt out any feelings. Shannon cast him a glance and held his gaze for just a moment longer than would someone without interest. Darin's shoulders relaxed. He waved as he smiled and felt at peace with God, Donna, and his living circumstances.

When Shannon and Miranda exited the door, Donna waited till they were out of ear shot and then turned to Darin.

"She is married and too old for you," Donna said.

"She is not that much older than me, and she may not be married for long," Darin responded with masculine authority.

By some genetic feat, Donna seemed to enlarge, and Darin stepped back.

"I will not have my boy pursuing a woman that is still tied in holy matrimony" Donna commanded.

Darin stepped back and paused.

"Will you help me when or if she becomes divorced?" Darin said, regaining some composure.

"If, and only if, there is no influence on her marriage by your meddling." Donna meant every word, and Darin knew that she was right if he wanted to call himself a Christian. Besides, Darin thought, how would he feel if some other man was looming over his own marriage.

"I will not encourage Shannon to sin, and I will not pretend to be her friend. I will wait to see what God does." Darin bound himself in an oath before his aunt, God and himself. The matter was dropped, and he assisted his second mother in cleaning up the kitchen and clearing the table.

Chapter 21

Wendsday morning came, and Darin didn't stir. He felt sick, uninterested, even rebellious. Thunderous stomps of late devotees pounded through the floorboards. Donna and Jimmy were running late. Every Sunday was stressful, and Darin was glad to be sitting out this one. Breakfast was always wolfed down. Donna never made it out the door before committing a mad search for a missing article of clothing.

Jimmy, ever calm, and never a pressuring husband, would wait unfazed by Donna's palpable tension. Darin did not know how he did it. Did he not care? Was he just along for the ride? Donna's demanding and domineering manner could really get under his skin. If she was his real mother, he was certain they would no longer be on speaking terms. Darin loved Donna because she took him in. Any character flaws that Darin observed in Donna were easily dismissed due to her voluntary sacrifice on Darin's account.

The door at the top of the stairs opened, and Donna yelled, "Darin...are you ready for church?"

With a large exhale that is characterized by overbearing repetition, Darin stood and walked to the bottom of the stairs.

"Remember, I don't feel well today," Darin said without sting but firmly.

Donna studied him a moment and calculated her response.

"We're gonna be late, hon," Jimmy blurted with perfect timing.

Jimmy's passive reminder pulled Donna back from her usual conflict with any family member attempting to escape corporate attendance to church.

"Fine, we will see you later then," Donna said with a slightly cutting tone as she shut the door unnecessarily.

Darin waited. Donna sometimes would change her mind and return with more force. Not today. She stomped off with Jimmy in tow and left for her Sunday. Darin won and smiled. He was going to have the whole morning to himself. Trowing on his robe, he started a pot of coffee and got the paper from the driveway as the it brewed.

He felt like a man, defying his commanding aunt, even though he had to lie just a little. He wasn't sick, but he didn't feel great about going to church. Seeing Shannon and her husband together even though he knew they were getting a divorce would upset him too much. It was better to be drinking coffee in silence, while he perused the paper for available places to rent. He had a job, a woman was attracted to him, and he would find a place of his own where he wouldn't be shoved away by a matriarch. It felt great to be in charge, to see a future carved out as he saw fit. Solely responsible for himself, master of his fate, and owner of his time.

The rentals were more expensive than he had imagined. His first duty as a man was to manage his finances. He thought the money he made working with Marty was good until he started budgeting what rent would be. He needed to ask Marty for a raise if he was to live on his own. Then he started looking at the addresses of some of these rentals. Currently Marty lived in a nearby trailer park, and it was no problem for Marty to swing by and pick him up and drop him off at home every day. The first step was most likely going to be transportation. Darin flipped to the for-sale section of the paper and started looming over vehicles he could afford. As Darin poured over the available trucks, cars, and vans for sale, a nagging thought entered his mind.

Why was he just now looking for a car? He was well over the legal age to drive. The other neighborhood kids had been zooming around for some time. Why didn't he have a car? Why hadn't he thought of this before? Genuine anger overtook Darin. Had Donna been holding him back? Could he even drive? His mind raced for answers, and his thoughts led him to a door that he was terrified of opening. He was crazy. The therapist had diagnosed him as anti-social, or was it schizoid? It did not really matter because Donna wouldn't have it, and the diagnosis was never discussed.

Why did he always forget that he was different? Why did he resent his aunt for mothering him, yet love her for providing for him? For too long he had been resigned to let his family usher him from age to age with little to no change. From now on he will take the medication that the therapist suggested. He would manage himself. He would show Jimmy and Donna that he could take care of himself.

Darin began to cry in his robe. Out of self-pity, out of a deeper acceptance of self-awareness. Coffee tasted bitter, and the paper became a tool of other men more capable. As Darin let out these subterranean emotions long held back by lack of examination, a warm thought pushed through. Jimmy and Donna would help him if he asked. Men asked for help and helped those around them. He could do that; he could be helped and help others. Adults do that, and Darin could humble himself in pursuit of independence.

Darin began by making a list. He needed a driver's license, a vehicle, more income and... He needed many things, Darin concluded, but the first step to independence would be a license. Darin found a phone book and searched for the number of the DMV. He called, and the phone rang and rang. After a mortal taste of eternity, an uninterested and dismissive voice answered: "Department of Motor Vehicles," the voice said.

"Umm, yes, I would like to get my driver's license," Darin informed the monotone low-level bureaucrat.

"Do you have a driver's permit?" the bland operator inquired.

"No, do I need a permit before getting a license?" Darin pressed.

"All motorists with no previously issued license need to obtain a driver's permit before they can be issued a license," the voice performed with no detectable originality or enthusiasm.

"How do I get my permit?" Darin asked, feeling entangled and disoriented.

"Come to the main office, get the permit packet, study it and then take the multiple-choice test. If you pass the test, you will be issued a permit." The voice waited.

"Ok, then I get my license?" Darin asked.

"After having your learners permit for at least six months before you can apply for a driver's license." The voice was clearly nearing its patience to remain on the call answering questions.

"Thank you," Darin said.

The voice hung up.

There are always invisible steps prior to real progress, Darin thought. If you want to eat you need to cook; if you want to cook, you need cooking utensils; if you have cooking implements you need to know how to use them. To do that you must have a stove and a home for that stove to be in. If you want the stove to work, you must pay for gas or electricity, and to do that you must have a job. To have a job, you must have a ride and the ability to work. If any of these is missing, you will not be able to eat.

Darin felt silly in his robe. He went downstairs and took a shower. When he was finished, he cleaned the kitchen and picked up the living room. When his work was finished, he waited. It was already past noon, and Jimmy and Donna were not back. They must have gone to lunch with friends. Hopefully everything is ok. Anxiety always built up in Darin when patterns shifted or expectations were not met. They did not say that they would be back right after church, thought Darin. Everything must be fine. Self-soothing by reframing what was true had little impact on his internal pressure, but it did create some space for him to think about other things.

He had been taught by his counselor how to limit his ruminations, but sometimes it felt like just a parlor trick. Where is my medication? Why are they not home? Maybe Donna has it in her room? Darin went into Jimmy and Donna's room and did some light probing. He felt guilty for invading their privacy, but she did have his medications, and they were his.

He opened a few drawers in Donna's nightstand and found some cash, which he left unmolested, and a worn Bible full of tabs and markings. There were a few other items of little interest. Darin went to Jimmy's side and found a pill container, but his excitement waned when he read the name on the prescription. What was wrong with Jimmy? Should I take one of his pills? Darin just wanted to fix his problem. He no longer wanted to be isolated, hamstrung, and lost. Better sense won and he left Jimmy's medication alone.

Darin moved to the bathroom and scoured every nook and cranny. He felt like an invader that was on a mission to retrieve stolen treasure. A mixing of guilt and authority left an uneasy feeling in his gut as his rummaging continued. Feminine products, dirty laundry, clean garments, gels, goos, implements, and ornaments. No medications. Darin was meticulous in his search, making sure to replace every article just as he had found it. Donna had an uncanny ability to know if something had been moved or misplaced. Defeated, Darin returned to the living room. Maybe if his mother and father were still here he wouldn't need medications, permits, and raises. Maybe everything would have been different.

Damn ruminations and obsessions. Just wait and ask them. Just sit still and be ok. Darin wanted to destroy the house to find his confiscated solution in pill form. He reframed and went to get his jacket. Muttering to himself Darin said, "I'll go on a walk. Movement always calms me down."

He put on his favorite sneakers and made his way out the main door and down the porch stairs. Walking wasn't a cure but when he moved, long walks felt like a temporal respite from his own internal agonies and anxieties. Rarely did he have a planned route. Often, he would find himself headed to quiet places. Since his mother died, he would go as if searching for her by the river, which was accessible from the park. As a child he had found a bridge. He would play or wait, daydream and forget under his bridge in the park. During the daytime there were few vagrants, and it was fun to play in the small creek that feeds the main river nearby.

His bridge was unique. The sounds of rumbling cars felt comforting; yet in their absence, the quiet of nature could be felt. There was an unintentional sequence of rhythmic vibrational sound and stillness. The creek babbled; the warmth of the sun enjoyed but with shelter. Concrete and forest, man and God, sound but dampened. The environment of the bridge gave Darin comfort.

As the years went on, he frequented the bridge less and less because the bums had become more feral. When he was a kid, there would only be one or two homeless men sleeping in tucked away enclaves. They always kept the bridge world neat and free of paraphernalia, unique to men that live without attachments. As time went on debris littered the bridge, and it made Darin feel like a world had been invaded and destroyed.

Darin always returned to his underworld despite knowing that it would be in disarray. The comfort that the bridge brought him as a child was not easily forgotten, and a lingering hope pushed him to continually be disappointed. Darin knew there would be broken bottles, smoldering fires, and discarded rubbish; yet he longed to experience a feeling that could never be recreated. As a teenager, he would push through the overgrown brush, spy the vagrants, and take inventory of the environment. He would usually leave and return to where the moms strolled, and the children skipped rocks.

This day was different. As he silently came through the foliage, he spotted a young kid. A blonde with dirty hair and strange

clothing was sitting in the dirt by a poorly built fire. The young man
was patting a bongo in a rhythm unlike music but somehow identi-
fiable to Darin. He could sense that the kid was newly forlorn and
adrift. Something in Darin pushed him to approach the wild- looking
stranger.

Unable to conceal his approach due to the thickness of the
bushes and the grass, the drummer turned to see what or who was
causing the disturbance. Darin emitted a genuine smile that he was unaccustomed to producing, and the boy returned warmth for warmth.
Instinctively, Darin came around the kid in a wide arch so as not to
invoke discomfort. Darin never liked it when people approached him
from directly behind. Even if Darin knew who it was, it made him
irritable and uncertain.

When Darin came within speaking distance of the kid he rested on his haunches.

"How is it going?" Darin asked with noticeable apprehen-
siveness.

"Good, man, how are you doing?" The newly dirty drifter
responded.

"I'm ok. I kind of had a rough day, and I like to come here
sometimes to think. My name is Darin, what's yours?" Darin extended his hand and then wished he hadn't because the boy's hands were
filthy.

"I'm Kai!" said the kid with a grandness.

Kai swung his arm wide and grabbed Darin's hand with
warmth, passion, and enthusiasm. Darin liked him immediately. His
shoes were worn, and his pants were loose. He wore faded tie-dye and
a hemp necklace with some sort of Celtic design. After a strong em-

brace, Kai's hands returned to his drum, and he followed the introduction with an upbeat drum riff. Darin noticed that there was an empty bottle of Boone's Farm near the kid, and he assumed that it had recently been consumed.

"Why are you having a bad day, bro?" Kai was pleased that Darin was not a weirdo or an officer of some type.

Darin laughed. He was having a bad day because he was dumb, incapable, late, unprepared, and in love with a woman that needed more than he could offer. It wasa holiday too, and mandatory cheeriness was hard to produce for Darin when he felt like he did today.

"I am having trouble getting my driver's license." Darin decided to summarize the reasons for his melancholy.

"Bro, why don't you have it already?" Kai asked with genuine curiosity that blunted the sharpness of his question.

"I've been really busy with my job, and I just did not need it till now," Darin answered and rested in his response realizing that it was mostly true.

"I don't have a license either, man, just these dogs," Kai said as he lifted a foot revealing holes on the bottom of his sneakers.

"Don't need gas, don't have to make payments, and they never break down!" Kai said with pride: "A man with nothing must summon or begin the process of dying."

Both the young men laughed. They were at the same place in the same situation even though they got there by different means. Kai had one eye that was a bit crazy. It made Darin slightly uneasy. He had a warm disposition, but the eye revealed that the kid was not entirely steady. Darin wondered if he had giveaways that were a window to his imbalances.

"Whatcha doing out here anyways?" Darin asked, tossing a pebble into the fire.

"Living free. Dude. What's it look like?" the drummer said as he looked at his empty bottle with visible disappointment. "What are YOU doing here?" inquired the wily eyed kid with the intention of rebalancing the pair's status.

"I come here to think sometimes. Like I said, it's kind of a bad day, and I feel better when I walk out here." Darin felt slightly ashamed for asking the kid what he was doing out here.

The kid was right to reestablish equality, Darin thought. It might be easier than one thinks to become a bum. If his aunt had not taken him in, then he might have ended up living under this bridge. He was no better than Kai, and he did mean to sound that way; but he realized quickly that his question did have judgement packaged as assumption.

"I'm sorry. I just meant how did you get here, not that you don't belong here," Darin said with humility.

"It's all good man. It's a legit question. I had to split. My pops and moms were getting weird with the God stuff, and I couldn't take it anymore," Kai said with veiled regret and open defiance.

"What kind of weird stuff?" Darin asked.

"Like cult stuff, man. The main church leader was an "THE END IS NIGH" type."

"You mean revelations? Or apocalypse?"

"Yeah, dude, but not just that. He was diddling a lot of the girls and had everyone convinced that he needed more wives before the end happened," Kai explained, growing agitated.

The young blonde kid reached inside his Baja hoodie's kangaroo pouch and revealed a pouch of Drum roll-your-owns. With deft fingers, he managed to roll a tight cigarette with the vestiges of the tobacco. He lit the smoke and visibly relaxed. Smokers always seem more at ease, Darin thought. He wished that he smoked, but he hated the smell, and it would be too much of a hassle to hide it from Donna.

"That's crazy about your family and that church," Darin said after accustoming himself to the stench of the cigarette.

"That's not even the worst of it. My parents volunteered my little sister to be his wife. I got pissed, and my dad and I came to blows. The church elders and my pops decided that I had to go," Kai said, while looking at the remnant of the pit fire.

"How old is your sister?" Darin asked.

"Like fourteen, dude!"

I thought my church was full of weirdos, but it looks like I was wrong," Darin confessed.

"Before my family got into the cult thing, I loved church, man; the music and the potlucks, and I got down with Jesus," Kai lamented.

"I go to a church with my family most Wednesdays," Darin said with some guilt.

"That's a good thing, dude. It's not God that's messed up, it's people!" Kai said, growing in animation and presence.

Darin thought about it and nodded his head in affirmation. He thought about the girl who he had almost killed with a rock a long time ago. Her dad had acted pious and pure, but if anyone had crossed him during the week, he was hell on wheels. It was like he never ironed a shirt or combed his hair before he went to church. Then Darin thought about all the drunks in AA. That was like a church, and they were a rotten bunch of great guys. All of them admitted being sinners and were genuinely trying to be good.

"I guess it's all right," Darin said.

"What kind of church do you go to?" Kai said with a smirk.

"I think it's nondenominational, whatever that means," Darin answered.

"That's a good thing, dude. Once the churches start getting funny names or jazzy leaders, then you have a problem," Kai said, flicking his cigarette away like it didn't just ease his tensions.

"Where are you staying now?" Darin asked.

Under this bridge, like the Billy Goat Gruff," Kai answered, pointing his fingers by his temples miming a goat.

"You want to stay at my place?" Darin asked before he concluded that he wanted to invite Kai.

"Yeah," said Kai.

"Okay," said Darin. "Well, we better get back to my house then because I need to make sure it's cool with my aunt," Darin said abashedly.

"Let me grab my bedroll," said Kai as he popped up and headed to the enclave tucked up where the road and abutment meet.

Darin knew the spot Kai had stashed his stuff; he had spent many an hour in that crevice as a kid but no longer felt comfortable because the spot had become frequented by vagrants. As fast as he was gone, Kai reemerged. His face was aglow. The two young men started walking to Darin's house like old friends that commuted daily together.

"By the way, man, if I'm going to be staying at your house

you should know that my real name is Joshua." The kid presented his hand like they hadn't already made introductions. Darin grasped his hand. "My name is still Darin," and the two laughed and made their way uninhibited.

By the time they got to Darin's house, the family car was parked in the driveway. Darin hadn't really thought this through. His aunt was not selfish, but she was wary of strangers. Perhaps today's service was about generosity, Darin thought, as the duo approached the steps to the main door. Darin got to the door first.

"Hey, ah Joshua, can you wait a second? I want to talk to my aunt and uncle and make sure it's all right if you stay," Darin said with some embarrassment.

"It's all good. I knew you were going to have to ask first," Joshua said with a smile.

Darin opened the door and smelled baking. His odds of gaining success were already in his favor. Donna looked up from her work and smiled at Darin until she remembered that he said he was ill.

"I thought you were sick?" Donna said, as her face morphed from contentment to parental disfavor.

"I was, but I went on a walk to feel better," Darin said in partial truth.

"Well, do you feel better? Are you hungry? I am making blueberry muffins," Donna said, reverting to her original state of tranquility.

"Yes, please!" Darin said, while glancing out the window at Kai.

"We got enough for a guest?" Darin asked.

With surprise, Donna looked up at Darin and instinctively

veered her gaze to the porch locating the rough-looking youngster.

"You got a friend out there, Darin?" Donna asked with suspicion and surprise.

"Yeah, I do. I met him on my walk. He needs some help, I think," Darin admitted.

Donna looked over to Jimmy, and then back at Darin, and said "Well, bring 'em in before the muffins get cold."

Chapter 22

Thursday morning came early ending the holiday. Reality moves faster than hope when we forget to be grateful. Kai was up before Darin and looked like a different person after showering, eating, and donning clean, borrowed clothes. Darin could hear Kai and Donna laughing upstairs. Stirring in his bed, Darin thought to himself that of course he was running behind on the day that he was going to ask for a raise. Beating off resistance, Darin launched up, got dressed, brushed his teeth, and rushed upstairs to eat and pack a lunch.

"Good morning, sunshine," Kai said, poking in good humor.

"Good morning, Kai" Darin responded in annoyance. Darin had called Marty the night before to ask if Kai could get some work with them. Marty was happy to have him since they needed the help.

"I made you guys lunch and coffee," Donna interceded, knowing her nephew did not do well to morning sarcasm.

"Thanks. I'll get up in time tomorrow. I just overslept for some reason," Darin said with a bit of coldness.

Darin was annoyed. How could he ask for a raise, get a driver's license, and help others if he couldn't even get out of bed in time. The night before he agreed to himself that he would be assertive. That he would lay out his clothes, prepare the coffee, and prepack their lunch. He did not do any of those things. He stayed up late, making deals with himself only to come up short on every agreement.

Being a man means more than having a male organ. It means discipline, responsibility, leadership, accountability, and dedication to God, family, and a purpose greater than self. That's what the pastor had said a few Sundays ago anyway, and the idea burrowed into Darin's mind and took up residence. However, knowing and doing are two different things. Doing requires more than just understanding. It demands commitment and sacrifice.

Darin swore to himself that he would go to bed earlier tonight and prepare before bed. Darin grabbed a coffee cup filled three quarters full of coffee and added cold water for the remaining quarter. He then gulped it down in an all-in-one long drink.

"That's one way to do it," Kai exclaimed.

A short blast of a vehicle horn interrupted the breakfast gathering.

"Better get going," Donna blurted. She was wearing her pink robe. Darin hated it for some reason. Something felt false. Donna was not a child, nor was she a creature of comfort. Perhaps it was the way Donna gave orders and hijacked leadership from under her floral patterns that got under his skin. Donna always knew what Darin needed to do, but Darin wanted to know what to do by himself.

His father was dead; and in his absence, he was left with a bossy woman robed in pink to guide him. He felt angry and bitter at Donna. He wanted her to let him figure it out. The only way to stop this cycle would be for him to assert himself and to rise first and make the coffee. Then he would be at the kitchen counter prior to the rest of the family.

The horn honked longer, and Darin abandoned his irritation.

"Let's go!" Darin said, as if it was Kai making him late.

The duo descended the stairs and braced themselves for the cold. It was unusually frosty, and Darin wished he had worn his jacket. Darin repressed the instinct to shiver and walked tall. As Kai and Darin approached the truck, Kai positioned himself to ensure that he would not have to sit in the middle. Another slight to his manhood, thought Darin. He let it go when he realized that he would be uncomfortable sitting right next to Marty since he was a stranger.

Darin entered first and sat in the middle. Kai followed and shut the door. Marty was smoking. He did not look irritated, but as always there was a feeling of impatience emanating from him.

"Can I get a smoke?" Kai asked.

Darin was embarrassed and had a difficult time hiding it. Marty handed Kai a cigarette and put the truck in reverse. Perfect, thought Darin. I'm sitting bitch between two smokers. At least the heat was on, but the windows were closed. Being smashed in the middle of a smoke-filled cab, on an empty stomach, with a caffeine rush hitting all at once filled Darin with angst.

Marty drove in silence for a while. Everyone seemed lost in their own thoughts. Drives to work are never filled with laughter and conversation like rides home from work can be.

"Listen up, fellas. The homeowner of the property we will be working at today is a bit off," Marty announced without customarily small talk.

Darin and Kai sat in silence.

"If she talks to you politely, direct any questions she may have to me. If you see her through a window, do not look at her."

"This is weird," Kai blurted.

"Yeah, she is a strange cat. But I think she is just lonely or crazy a little," Marty said in a calm manner. "She likes attention. Yet, when she gets it, she acts offended. I don't really know why; I just know the job pays well and we are almost done," Marty explained.

"Broads..." Kai added.

Marty pulled out two smokes and handed one to Kai. They seemed to be developing a bond that Darin and Marty lacked. Darin almost asked for a cigarette but did not want the others to think he was just trying to fit in. Kai and Marty lit up, and Darin could tell that Kai was used to early mornings and work.

"Listen, just leave her be and avoid looking at her," Marty reinforced.

Just as Darin was accustomed to the smoke and the awarded middle seat, the trio arrived at the house. Lake Oswego looked much different in the morning than any of the other parts of the city. There were walkers and healthy dogs pulling on leashes. Yards were maintained, full of blooming trees and bushes. New cars looked cleaner with moisture on them, whereas the old beaters in the other neighborhoods looked worse when wet. How can wealth make damp mornings seem richer? Darin thought as they pulled into the driveway.

"Oh, and do NOT throw your cigarette buts on the property. Crush them out and put them in your pocket or the trash," Marty said with clear authority.

The three men exited the truck, and Marty explained to Kai

which tools he would be using: mostly a post hole digger and a shovel. Kai was smiling and appeared eager to earn some money and work.

Darin watched the house to see if he could spot Melissa's location. Sure enough he noticed a curtain moving and saw her fingers holding back the fabric. There she was. What happened to this lady, thought Darin. How is it that a lady like that can live in a house like this? The idea that wealthier people were better than poor people was being challenged in Darin's mind. Everyone is crazy, though Darin and monopoly money can't protect them from the madness that threatens us if we lose our way.

Darin almost pitied Melissa, but it's hard to "live and let live" when someone is actively trying to sabotage you. Darin just wanted to work; he did not want to avert his natural awareness. He did not want to act like things were normal when things were weird. Marty took the young men to the back of the property and lined out where the new post holes would need to be dug for the fence installation. Once Kai and Darin started working, Marty left.

Kai worked hard and kept up his energy with each hole he dug. Darin was impressed and a little ashamed that Kai worked harder than him. Darin now realized that Marty was doing him a favor. Marty could hire other men to do more and pay less, but he was being kind to Darin. Emotion stirred in Darin. He felt loved, but he didn't want to be coddled. Darin exhorted more effort and worked harder than he ever had before. As he picked up the intensity, Kai smiled and worked even harder too.

Feelings of insecurity vanished as the two dug like dogs hiding bones. Darin liked the competition and realized Kai thrived off it too. The sun broke the haze and blue commanded the sky. Kai looked like a man, not a runaway. His presence was calm and joyful. Darin saw "Joshua" instead of "Kai," the drummer that liked booze and bridges. Darin wondered if he looked like his friend, and hoped he did, but came to accept that however he felt inside didn't change what was happening on the outside. He was a hard worker; he was a man, and he deserved to feel good about himself and his labor.

When Joshua and Darin took a natural pause in their effort they heard shouting. They both looked at each other and dropped their tools to go and identify the source of the screaming. When they reached the front of the house, they saw a giant man and a truck loaded with fence material. Marty was angry, throwing up his hands and pacing.

"Look, Al, I need that lumber. I can't pay you back until I get paid," Marty said after he calmed himself down.

"Hehe, that's what you said last time buddy," Al sneered in a quiet but menacing way.

"I know I owe you money; I know there were times that I fell short. But I am on the wagon now and have been for some time. I will give you the title to my truck as collateral to guarantee payment." Marty said with authority.

"This piece of shit?" Al said as he lazily pointed to Marty's truck.

"Yeah, this piece of shit. It looks rough, but it runs good, and I haven't had a problem with it," Marty said with finality.

Al ran his thumbs under the straps of his suspenders holding up his massive trousers. He looked at Darin and smiled. There was something familiar in that look. Darin had heard about Al; he knew that he was not a man to be messed with. When Al gazed at him, he did not avert his stare but held his look and returned the threatening coldness. Al smiled again and moved towards Marty's truck. He slowly walked around it, doing some sort of calculation. When he made his way full circle, he stopped right in front of Marty, purposefully invading personal space.

"You're off the sauce?" Al asked.

"I am now, for over six months," Marty replied, sterling in truth.

"Alright boys, unload the truck," Al said as he pulled Marty to the side.

Marty gave a nod to Darin and Joshua. Joshua looked at Darin, and they moved towards Al's truck to begin unloading it. As they worked, Darin kept an eye on Marty. He saw Marty get the title out of his truck and hand it to Al. The two men shook hands and parted. Al got back in his truck, and Marty started helping unload the materials. Darin jumped in the back and started handing boards to Joshua and Marty. As he was grabbing the last board, he instinctively looked at the rearview mirror.

He had felt Al's stare and met his eyes without knowing he would. He felt Al's consciousness penetrate his being. Darin was exposed but not threatened, and he looked back at Al. There was a clear understanding between the two men. A wolf knows his own kind. A predator knows if it's looking at prey or a threat. Darin was keenly aware that Al was a killer, just like the sky was blue.

When the truck was unloaded, Marty slapped the side of Al's truck. The husky man with fleshy lips muttered something and slowly pulled out of the driveway.

"Let's get back to work," Marty said with ardent eyes.

Darin avoided eye contact with Joshua. He was embarrassed for his uncle. The rest of the day went by in quiet toil. There are moments when the only way through is by sweat. Not metaphysical or philosophical but pure physical exertion. The three men cut boards, hauled Quickrete for the posts, and hammered nails with precision and tenacity. Melissa continued to peer out from curtains or parade past windows with alluring gestures, but the men ignored her. She was nothing more than a distraction. The men were following Marty's lead and not succumbing to lust or curiosity.

"That woman is a Siren," Marty said.

Joshua and Darin looked at each other in confusion.

"What's a Siren?" Joshua asked, unashamed of not knowing something.

"In Greek mythology it was a feminine creature that would put men under a spell at sea and make them crash their boats," Marty explained.

"How did they do that?" asked Joshua, while still working.

"By some sort of magic, or by their inherent lure. Either way, men could not pay attention to them or lose their lives if they were caught by their songs," Marty added. "Keep working, men, and do not be swayed by the song of the Siren!" Marty said with animated facial expressions, but in a quiet tone.

In all the years Darin had worked with Marty, he had never heard him reference "Greek Mythology. Ever since Marty got involved with AA, he had become a smarter and more reliable man. Darin bet Marty didn't even know where he had heard about Sirens. Darin logged the story away because he liked it and wanted to remember the parable.

Melissa's husband came home at the same time the three men had finished the work. Marty and Joshua were cleaning up the jobsite, and Darin was loading up the truck with some trash and tools. Melissa's husband was tall and walked with his hips forward. Darin did not like him. He could feel the man's feminine passive aggressiveness and arrogance just by seeing him exit his car and walk to the front door.

Darin waited to see if the man would acknowledge him, but he didn't to Darin's relief. This tall, skinny, slack-wearing beta, masquerading as a cubicle alpha, represented everything about the well-off that Darin had disdain for. It was better to avoid communication and let Marty talk to him, Darin thought. Darin finished loading the tools as the temperature began to dip. He was beginning to get cold now that the labor had ceased, and his sweat had made him wet.

Marty and Joshua came around to the front of the house. Marty said something to his new friend and then pointed to Darin or the truck. Joshua made his way to Darin, looking content and tired. Marty approached the front door and knocked. The two boys watched as Marty talked with the owner of the house. Darin could perceive that the tall man was a bit annoyed. He left and, in a few moments, came back with his jacket.

Marty and the corporate slave went around the property. It was funny watching Marty lead him around while the tall fellow pretended to understand or even care about what Marty was explaining to him. After what seemed like a long time, the men returned to the front of the house. The man disappeared into his dwelling and reappeared in a few moments with a check in hand.

Marty turned and with a wide grin made his way to the truck. Joshua and Darin were already in the vehicle but had not started it.

Marty hopped in and cranked the ignition. It didn't start. Unfazed, Marty performed some sort of mechanical incantation and cranked it again. The old white work truck started, to Joshua and Darin's relief.

"Thank God," Marty said, with a big sigh of relief.

"Did he pay up in full?" Darin asked.

"He sure did!" said Marty, handing Joshua a Marlboro.

Joshua received the smoke with gratitude and lit up. In an instant Darin could see that the young guy was lost in thought now that he had a cigarette.

"After I drop you guys off, I can pay back Al and get that viper off my back," Marty said.

"How much do you owe Al?" Darin asked.

"None of your damn business," Marty said, only half joking. "Enough that I want to be done with him and all his kind," Marty added to round off his previous sharpness.

"Marty?" Darin blurted.

"Yeah?" Marty acknowledged, while taking a long drag.

"I would like to get a raise so I can get my driver's license and a car." Darin squeezed out his request feeling like there wasn't going to be a good time to ask this day.

"About time, son, about time," Marty replied without inflection.

"Does that mean I'll get a raise?" Darin pressed sheepishly.

"You will. I don't know how much yet. I've got to look things over. But you'll get a raise," Marty said as he flicked his exhausted smoke out the window.

Chapter 23

Joshua hung up the phone. He looked happy.

"Bro! My pops is leaving the church I was telling you about,"
Joshua said, gleaming. "I can't believe it. I kept telling him they were a
sham, but he was convinced that he needed to be 'obedient,' and that
I was arrogant and spiritually proud," Joshua continued.

"That's great news, man. Are you going to go back home?"
Darin asked with mixed feelings.

"I don't know bro; I mean I like working with you and Marty, and your aunt is awesome. But I can't stay here forever," Joshua
explained more thinking aloud rather than deciding.

"What about your sister? Did they make her marry the pastor
guy?" Darin asked, regretting his curiosity immediately.

"No, they didn't. Turns out that pastor was caught sleeping
with some other women that were not his wives. Everything started to
fall apart after that," Joshua said.

Both boys sat in silence in the living room. They had grown
close, and they were going to miss each other. Neither of them wanted to say what they both knew was ahead. Joshua was right; Donna

was generous, but his stay was temporary. Darin was shocked that she let him stay at all. The sermon at church the day when Darin had brought Joshua to the house must have been about taking care of the poor and needy.

Darin also hadn't made many friends in his life. He was different in many ways; sometimes distant and thoughtful, other times highly emotional and overwhelmed. Donna and Jimmy were both older too, so they did really get excited about doing kid stuff. In short, his childhood was isolated and overshadowed by grief and loneliness. It was true that he was not alone, but proximity to people is no substitute for real intimacy. Joshua was the first guy that Darin had made real friends with.

The friendship had started too late, however. Darin wanted to get his own place and pursue Shannon. He needed to show her and his family that he could take care of her and himself without the help of Donna. Darin was accelerating out from a prolonged childhood and into sudden manhood. He had to let Joshua go and get to work preparing himself for his future.

"Eugene is not that far away, and when I get my license I can come and visit you," Darin said, believing that he would but knowing deep down that it was probably not true.

God had been there for Joshua and Darin that day. Darin felt bad about skipping out on church. But now he saw that it was God all the time directing his steps. And he was proud that he was able to help Joshua, even if it was only for a few weeks. Darin realized that God would help him too if he needed it. Perhaps it was God all along that had been helping him. Donna and Jimmy couldn't have kids, and Darin remembered how he used to get upset about it when he was younger.

"How are you going to get home?" Darin asked, breaking the silence.

"Greyhound bus, dude!" Joshua said with a wide grin.

Darin had never been on a bus. When he went to school he walked. And his family never used public transportation. Part of Darin wished that he could go with Joshua on the trip.

"Is that how you got up to Portland?" Darin asked, forgetting his regret at the thought of Joshua leaving.

"You know it! A fella can go anywhere in the U.S.A if he has a little cash and a lot of patience."

Both boys laughed and thought of themselves as adventurous men, making their own destiny.

Donna came into the house and started washing her hands in the kitchen sink. She had been messing around with the flower beds. Every year she planted flowers, and every year they struggled to grow. Jimmy said if it was not for the Northwest climate, Donna couldn't grow grass. Donna was determined to have a green thumb; it was almost a need rather than a desire.

"What are you two up to today?" Donna said loudly over the running sink.

"Joshua is going home soon," Darin answered, matching her volume.

"No, bro. I'm going home today. Buses run continually, and I need to get back ASAP!" Joshua clarified.

Darin gulped. He felt a shock run through him. He was prepared for Joshua to leave, but not today.

Life was like that, dreary and monotonous, then sudden and

full of upheaval.

Donna turned off the water and gave the boys her full attention.

"What about that cult - I mean church - that they were a part of?" She inquired with genuine concern.

"That's done. My old man left the church and wants me to come home. He even said he was sorry. My dad never apologizes, but he did." Joshua was brimming with joy as he explained the dynamics to Donna.

Donna feigned a smile. Joshua did not detect her masked disbelief, but Darin did.

"It's true. He just got off the phone with his dad," Darin added to bolster his friend's confidence.

Darin could tell that Donna had mixed feelings. It was true that she was not maternal in the classical sense, but she was protective. The three sat for a moment, Donna studying Joshua, Darin watching Donna, and Joshua smiling with growing energy.

"When are you going to leave?" Donna asked

"I gotta go today," Joshua responded.

"I see. Do you need a ride somewhere?" Donna asked, unfazed by shifting tides.

"Oh, thanks, Auntie!" Joshua said with gratitude.

Donna even blushed a bit at Joshua's family pretense. Joshua did adapt well with Darin's family. It even bothered Darin a bit. They all seemed to like him instantly. He had always found it difficult to connect with any of them without some agitation. Not Joshua! He fit right in and assumed a role within a few days of his arrival. Joshua was a likable guy, and Darin dismissed any feeling of jealousy.

Joshua popped up and announced that he needed to get packed. Donna and Darin remained sitting in the living room.

"You did a good thing helping him out, Darin," Donna confessed once Joshua descended the stairs to the basement.

"Thanks," replied Darin, a little embarrassed.

"The bible says that when you help a stranger in need you are serving God." Donna gave Darin a smile and got up and walked to her bedroom.

Darin sat a minute. Everything was happening so fast. He was sad, happy, and felt unbalanced. Others seemed to move with the flow. He, however, found it difficult to change on a dime. Sudden changes gave him an upset stomach and often tongue-tied him. Darin sat alone for a moment, thinking about how he had met Joshua. He was happy that his family was going to be reunited. If his mom or dad called him back home, he would go too. Home is not a place, Darin thought. It is a feeling of connection. Joshua had one to return to, and Darin had to build one.

Donna drove the boys to the Greyhound station. Darin was intimidated by the logistical experience. They had to park, then wait in the right line. Then they got a ticket for Joshua. After that, they had to locate the right bus and stand again.

"Do you have our number written down?" Donna asked

"Oh, dang, good call," Joshua said as he snapped his fingers before digging out a notebook littered with drawings and poems.

Donna gave him the number, and Darin asked Joshua to write his number down on a piece of paper.

The boy handed the number to Darin and turned his head to the bus. The driver had alerted the would-be passengers that they would be departing soon. Some people hesitate and soak up all the lingering feelings; others move and are severe. There is no wrong way to change, but change we must. Darin admired Joshua's grit (he was young after all). Who knew what the ride would be like? Joshua wasn't afraid. Darin would have been dreading the upcoming unknowns, such as who would sit by him? What if he needed to go to the bathroom? What if he missed his stop? What if the bus driver fell asleep? Then the driver announced that the ticket holders could board the bus. Darin almost began to cry. Donna grabbed Joshua and gave him a hug. Then he looked at Darin and stuck out his hand. The two shook hands in a serious manner, then grinned and hugged. Joshua grabbed his bag, boarded the bus, and sat where Donna and Darin could not see him.

"Well, that's that then" Donna said, turning her head to look at Darin.

Darin continued to try and spot Joshua on the bus but could not locate him.

"Let's go. He will be fine" Donna said, while patting Darin on the back.

Just when they turned to leave, they heard Joshua.

"When you get your car give me a shout," Joshua said with his head squeezing through the window that would only open a little.

"I will!" Darin shouted while waiving.

Joshua shut the window and was gone. Darin smiled and started making plans to make his own journey to Eugene. Donna smiled and started walking to the car. They both got in and drove home. The world felt smaller without Joshua's gregarious nature, but it was nice to have some quiet. Darin looked out the window and the drive home went by like a dream.

When they got home, Donna told Darin that dinner would be ready in a couple of hours. He went down to his room and started to pick up the mess that Joshua left behind. He was a sloppy guy, always on the move and never picked up after himself. Darin hated that about him but felt sorry that he was gone. Dirty laundry needed to be washed, empty cups needed to be brought to the kitchen, and the floor needed vacuuming. Darin rarely had to clean his room; he was meticulous in keeping it clean. More so out of laziness rather than tidiness. If he did not make a mess, then he would not have to clean one up.

Some people are moving fast, soaking up all that life has to offer them. They bounce from one room to another, making messes and feel no disorder. They can eat and leave their plate, find the right outfit, and leave the discarded articles laying on the floor as they bounce out the door to meet the day. Living with Joshua this way frustrated Darin, but Joshua would tell him to "lighten up, man; it doesn't matter." In the grand scheme of things, Darin supposed that a little chaos did not matter.

He continued to clean up his room and bathroom with gratitude instead of frustration. While cleaning up the bathroom, Darin noticed a crucifix that belonged to Joshua. It was tarnished but still glowed. He picked it up and put it on. Darin agreed with himself that he would call Joshua and ask him for his address later. In the meantime, he would wear it. Darin felt closer to God that day, and he was proud of serving Him.

Two hours had gone by, and like clockwork dinner was ready. Donna was always on time, and so were Darin and Jimmy. The three sat like empty nesters, with only Jimmy maintaining his common nature. Both Donna and Darin were more quiet than usual.

"You know it's better that he went home," Jimmy said as he gnawed on his steak.

"I know, but I hope he is going to be ok," Donna said as she moved the food around on her plate.

"He will be fine. That boy has got some gusto," Jimmy said, keeping his focus on his food. Darin decided that he needed "gusto" too, and he would be bolder. Joshua had taught him to act instead of ruminating.

"He is probably home right now," Darin said.

"It's a good thing to be home," said Jimmy, smiling warmly to both his wife and Darin.

They returned his smile and started to eat.

When dinner was over, Jimmy got up and gave Donna a big kiss. She blushed and melted in his arms. Jimmy had a way of disarming her hardened exterior. Darin admired that about Jimmy.

"That was good cooking, dear," Jimmy said as he pinched Donna's side. "What about Sir? Are you ready to defend yourself?" Jimmy said with jollity, looking toward his adopted son.

Darin knew what that meant. Jimmy wanted to play Stratego. "I'm red!" Darin declared.

"Red or blue, it's gonna be sad for you!" Jimmy said as he pointed at Darin.

Chapter 24

"It isn't pretty, but it's been modified with an upgraded engine and some performance parts," said the potbellied man with a green tinted visor.

Darin looked at the man and nodded but he did not believe anything the salesman was saying. Sales guys just talk and talk; they never know. It's their job to make you question yourself and get a man second guessing himself. Darin wished Marty was here with him. Unfortunately, Marty had to work and could not make it to the lemon lot as he had agreed to. Marty told Darin that if he wanted to wait till the weekend then he could go. Darin was tired of walking and wanted a car.

How hard could it be? Darin thought. If it looked good and sounded good that was about all a regular guy could discern. It's exhausting trying to understand everything. Over the years hanging out with Marty on the jobsite, Darin had met these kinds of guys. They can fix damn near about anything, and you can almost feel them judging you when you don't know what they are talking about. Darin did not have a clue about cars. Marty had told him to make sure the oil on the dipstick was not jet black, and that there were no leaks on the ground. Marty also said it's a bad sign if it doesn't start right up when you crank it.

Darin and Marty had noticed a Ford Pinto on the lot a few days back, and it was in Darin's price range. He liked the Chevy Novas better because they looked powerful and dramatic. Cars like that were out of his reach, but he told himself that he would buy the car he really wanted later. For now, he needed transportation. Begging for rides or waiting until Donna wanted to go somewhere was getting old. Marty said Ford Pintos are reliable and economical.

"You want to take her for a spin?" asked the lot attendant.

"I do," said Darin

"Well hold on a minute, and I'll get the keys," said the portly man as shuffled to the main office.

The heat was burdensome, Darin was sweating, and it was making him uncomfortable. This was it. If the car ran well, he would buy it. Darin remembered everything Marty had taught him about driving. Driving this Pinto would be different than driving the work truck. Darin sharked around the car and inspected it like an alien would a new planet. There were spots of rust, and the rims were blackened by use.

The lights were intact, and the seats looked like they were in okay condition. He wished he knew more about engines and transmissions, but he kept scrying the Ford despite his lack of mechanical astuteness. The salesman was making his way back to Darin, and he was sweating heavily now. His white shirt was wet, and he labored under his own rotund build.

"You got a license?" asked the man.

"I do, here." Darin handed the man his license like a spy handing a custom agent a fake passport.

Darin waited apprehensively as the man copied information off Darin's license to his sheet of paper on a clipboard. Then the man pulled a license plate out hidden under his clipboard. He walked to the back and stuck the plate onto the vehicle.

"Every car has got to have a plate on it," said the man, aware of Darin's curiosity.

"You can take it out of the lot, turn right, and stay on the main road. After a mile or so, there will be a place where you can make a U-turn at a light. Flip it around and head back," the man continued.

The man extended his arm and dangled the keys, free for the taking. Darin seized them like a young Arthur removing Excalibur from the stone. Darin opened the door and studied the interior. He loved the way the gauges looked and how the car smelled. Oil, leather, and chromed steel, Darin felt right, like a man that could go places and decide things. Freedom was moments away. If only the car runs well, this dream could be real.

When Darin turned the ignition, the car cranked but did not start. The salesman knocked on the window, and Darin rolled it down. He leaned close, and the green haze from his visor made the moment seem foreign.

"Pump the gas; it hasn't started yet. Give her three pumps and then turn it," said the man with a smile Darin could not discern.

"Got it," Darin said.

He knew about pumping gas before starting. Marty's truck never started on the first crank, whether it had been recently running or not.

Thump, thump, thump, crank, rumble.

It was like seeing a woman naked for the first time. He was enthralled. He wanted to sit in its glory, touch everything and keep it for himself. The rumble of the engine, the promise of freedom, and the symbol of manhood all in one sensation. The used car salesman was grinning ear to ear, and Darin felt embarrassed. He had lost any ability to act indifferent. To don a poker face later would be silly. Everyone knew that he wanted the car. The impatience of the lot attendant grew, and he waved to Darin to go.

He put the car in drive and made his way through the lot. Traffic was not bad, and he only had to let three cars go by before he could turn out of the lot without pressure. When Darin turned onto the road, there was a faint squeal.

"Damn it," Darin said to himself.

After he got away from the dealership, he let it rip. Pedal to the metal, The Pinto responded and aggressively accelerated. Darin laughed and slowed down. He wanted to know if the car had any spice. If it did not jump when he hit the gas, he did not care how great it ran. Cars have to have a bang to them. Who cares if it's affordable and economical if there is no pop. Darin wondered why the guy who modified it was selling it. The car was fast and cheap. Was this luck? Was there something Darin was missing?

Bam, he hit the accelerator again and the vehicle sprung forward. The engine made sounds that Darin had only heard as a pedestrian. Hearing powerful cars pass by him as he walked would be a thing of the past after today. The spot to make the U-turn appeared quickly, and Darin had to almost slam on the breaks to not blow by. He made the turn, and he heard the squeal again. Something about turning was making a bad sound. Darin made a mental note to ask the sales guy about the sound when he returned to the lot.

Darin had to wait for several cars to pass by before he dashed across the road in the dark green Pinto. There was the noise again as he turned. It did not matter if it was left or right; when he turned the car, it squealed. This really bothered Darin. Normally Pintos are slow and sluggish, but this one, to his delight, had been fitted with a bigger engine. He felt so lucky to find something he could afford that also had some grit to it. But the damn thing was making noise and not starting on the first crank. Darin did not want to make emotional decisions. He did not want to imagine things were good when the evidence showed that they were not.

"She's got the some bang!" said the lot lizard.

Darin blushed a bit then focused on the squealing. "I do like how she runs, but every time I turned the wheel there was a horrible noise."

"Ahh... it just needs the power steering topped off. Hold on a minute." The man pulled a radio off his belt and told someone on the other end to come to him with some power steering fluid ASAP.

A young guy in a greasy blue jumpsuit came running with a rag in one hand and a yellow bottle in the other. The man with the green visor pointed to the Pinto without even looking at the kid. With no hesitation to be commanded, the young man popped the hood, found the power steering reservoir, and topped it off.

"Anything else, boss?" asked the young guy with resigned eyes.

"Yeah, check the carburetor and see if it needs adjusting," replied the man, who was used to telling others what to do, without pleasantries.

"Let Hal here tinker with the carburetor again, and you will see she will start right up. As far as the sound it was making, it was only because the fluid was low." the sales guy pulled out a cigar and lit it in a way Darin had never seen before. He kept the flame near but not touching the cigar. As he held the lighter, he rotated the large dark smoke.

Cigar smokers seemed like a different species than cigarette smokers. They took a certain pleasure in the ceremony, in the addiction, as if they embodied what it meant to smoke more than just crave the stimulant and cave to its call. Cigarette smokers seemed forced, pressured, almost slave- like. Cigar smokers seemed in control, wise and indifferent to the opinions of others. The smell of cigars is overwhelming, intruding, and it bellows. The smell of cigarette smoke is sharp and nasty, but it extinguishes quickly, giving the non-smoker forced to be in the company of the addict respite.

Darin watched the man with trepidation. He knew that he was at his mercy. He wanted the car, and he would almost believe whatever the man told him if the car would be his.

"Well, what do you think?" Inquired the seasoned salesman.

"I'll buy it if that noise is fixed. My uncle's truck needs pumping to start too. I'm not too worried about that," Darin confessed to relieve himself of any tension of pretending to haggle. The man laughed and smiled.

"Look son, it's a decent car at a fair price. It has been modified as you can tell when you drove it. That means there may be problems with it that I don't know. Pintos are cheap, and the guy that sold this to me was in a bind. Normally cars with modifications sell for more.

But I can't guarantee it, you see?" the man explained to Darin's surprise.

"It's good to go, boss!" yelled the kid in the blue jumpsuit.

Darin smiled. "I want to buy the car, sir."

"Yeah, I thought you would. Follow me to the office, and we will write it up."

The man walked slowly, and Darin found it difficult to maintain the slow saunter. He wanted to rush, move fast, and be done. Laying claims and owning are two different things. There is a period when you want to own something, but you don't. That is irksome.

The man walked past the ashtray by the door without extinguishing his smoke, and Darin braced himself to endure the inescapable suffocating aroma once inside. The man took Darin to a back room, pointed to the seat meant for customers, and pulled out a stack of papers. Darin signed several documents pretending to comprehend what they meant. He counted out the money for the car, and the man gave him the title and keys.

"She is all yours. You made a good deal today. Good luck son!"

The men shook hands, and Darin escaped the office, free of the vapors and owner of a future.

The drive home was fueled with imagination. The possibilities seemed endless. He could now work anywhere because he could drive. He could move out of Portland, or even out of the state of Oregon. The purchase of the Pinto had a molting effect on Darin. He was vulnerable now, with a new car, learning to drive, and his savings depleted. If he did not crash the vehicle and there were no mechanical issues, he would be independent and stronger soon.

The force conjured by the modified Pinto was impressive. The other motorists took notice and smiled or waved to Darin. He was not used to attention. Most of his life he had been grey, almost invisible to his peers. Something about mobility and horsepower shed the remnant of shyness and boyhood. Attention felt good, but Darin did not want to be like other young men he knew that got cars before him.

Some of the older kids that he knew acted like assholes when they got their first car. His memory turned to Kent, a short, ugly boy with fat fingers. His dad bought him an old Firebird that they restored together. As soon as the car was operational, Kent was speeding around with dice hanging in the mirror while wearing a letterman jacket. Kent was an absolute douchebag, but he seemed to be unaware of being judged and avoided. Perhaps the Firebird insulated him from the judgments of others. It mattered little. Darin did not want to be like that kid.

If it were not for Marty, Darin would not even have been able to get his driver's license or his new car. Marty let Darin drive to work after picking him up from Donna's. For months Darin got to drive the work truck to the jobsites and to the lumber yard. Marty taught him how to check his mirrors, merge into traffic, and avoid road rages. After he got his raise, Donna let him save even more so that he could buy a car.

Marty must have talked to Donna, because she was adamant that Darin help pay the bills. After Darin talked with Marty about wanting to buy a car and get his own place, Donna helped Darin manage a savings account and stopped asking him for money monthly. If he was saving for a car, he did not have to contribute money to the family. Purpose and gratitude filled Darin as he accelerated on the highway. He didn't feel like a fatherless boy, but rather a man on the verge of greatness.

However, even men of renown need gas when their tank is empty. The fuel indicator turned on, and Darin's daydreaming was smashed when he realized that he only had a few dollars left. Darin pulled into a gas station, and an attendant asked him how much gas he wanted in his car. Darin sifted through his pockets and told the greasy boy to put in two dollars and forty-five cents. Assuming correctly that there would be no tip, the attendant added the fuel with noticeable irritation.

It was true that he was broke, but he was not without prospects. Darin disliked the gas station employee for contributing to the dismissal of Darin's futuristic imaginations.

"Next time I get gas, I'll tip. I just bought the car today," Darin confessed to the attendant.

The boy looked at him and nodded. Clearly the kid lived off the here and now, not "next times." Darin let it go. He did not have more money, and he needed all of what was left to get home. As soon as the kid shut his gas flap, he started it up on the first crank. Pride took back its place, and Darin left the station forgetting the forlorn attendant.

As he pulled into the driveway of his house, he felt like a victor back from battle. A rite of passage had been completed, and Darin had emerged victorious. Jimmy came out the front door with a shit-eating grin on his face and quickly descended the stairs from the second floor living room. Darin was glad to be met with the excitement of Jimmy. Darin pulled in behind Donna's car and turned off the engine.

"Oh, boy, you got your wheels now!" Jimmy's excitement was genuine.

"What do you think?" asked Darin proudly.

"I love it; dark green is badass," Jimmy said as he made a lap around the parked Pinto.

"It's got a modified engine, too," Darin exclaimed.

"Really!?" Jimmy said, aglow.

"Yeah, she really gets up and goes!" Darin added.

"Well don't tell your aunt. Let her think it's just a regular slow Pinto!" Jimmy said, pointing to the hood.

Darin got packed in and struggled to find the hood release lever. Jimmy came over with a silly smile and immediately located and pulled the hood release. To Jimmy's surprise, under the hood was not a 2.0 stock engine with a better carburetor or intake manifold, but a 302 V8 engine.

"Holy crap, Darin! This thing has got a V8 in it!" Jimmy said, admiring the mechanical prowess it must have taken to install the larger engine in the smaller car.

Darin did not know exactly what Jimmy meant, but he knew it was good, and he felt even more proud.

Chapter 25

Darin decided that if he was going to get a chance to pursue Shannon, he would have to attend church more. He believed in God but did not like the songs and the group. Often, he felt like an outsider, but he couldn't shake it. If God wanted him to be different, he would have made him different, Darin decided. The regulars at the church had an air of superiority that was either real or imagined due to Darin's guilt.

Darin found it difficult to get close to Shannon during the sermon, but just seeing her at least eased his anguish. When their eyes would meet, she would smile but never seemed to make herself available for approach. Darin did not know what to do. Miranda and Donna were talking after the service, and Darin smiled at Shannon again. Again, she returned the smile but then turned her attention back to her mother and Donna.

Darin was starting to think that maybe she was just being polite; maybe she did not like him like he wished. She was, after all, a few years older, and he still lived in his aunt's basement. Finally, after he could not take it anymore, he decided to ask Donna her opinion.

This was the last resort. She was not the type of woman that approved of sinful lust. He would have to make it clear that he intended to marry her. That he didn't just find her attractive, but that he felt he should be her husband and she, his wife.

Darin planned it out and decided to ride with her to church instead of driving himself. After a few weeks of service attendance, he made his move on the drive home.

"Shannon is divorced now?" Darin blurted.

"You know she is, the poor child," Donna lamented.

"Well, do you think I could talk to her now?" Darin pressed.

"What about, Darin?" Donna stated as if to head off any approach before it began.

Darin was getting angry. Donna knew that he liked her, that he was attracted to her. For some reason, she dismissed his feelings. He wasn't a boy anymore. Why did she not realize this, like Jimmy and Marty did?

"I want to see her become my wife!" Darin almost screamed in frustration.

Donna was shocked and held the steering wheel with earnestness. Both her and Darin sat in the car, shocked by Darin's outburst. He had never said something like this before.

"Don't you think you're a little young to be talking about being married?" Donna finally uttered after an awkward silence.

Darin's frustration grew, but he found a way to master it and took some deep breaths. His aunt had known for some time that he wanted to talk to Shannon. Donna never made any effort to help him or set up gatherings he could be a part of. She resisted him getting a car and convinced him to stay in the basement until he was older. She said it made good financial sense because the economy was not doing so hot. She was stopping him from being a man.

"I do not think that I am too young to be a husband," Darin said in a confronting manner.

Taken aback, Donna composed herself.

"She has already divorced once, and she is the daughter of my good friend. Plus, you're different, Darin." Donna revealed her true feelings.

"I don't care that she has been divorced. That doesn't make her damaged goods. And what do you mean I am different?" Darin responded, with growing emotion.

They both knew what she meant. He spent hours alone, said little, and seemed to have a hard time functioning in the world without the help of his family.

"Well, Darin, ever since your mom died, I've taken care of you. Your mother made me promise that I would protect you. I have taken that promise seriously, and you should show more respect."

The same old story, Darin thought. It was the extra care that had hamstrung him. He was never encouraged to play sports or do things on his own. Ever since the slide incident and the therapist's intervention, Donna had been babying him. She was ruled by fear and by her controlling nature. If she isolated him, he would not be hurt. If she protected him from the world, she would keep her promise to her sister.

"You kept your promise, and I am grateful for it. I am a man now and I need you to see it. Your promise to my mom is holding me back." Darin's eyes filled with tears as he uttered the truth.

Donna's face started to contort, and Darin was not sure how

it would go after what he had just said. She could explode, or she could hear him and be calm. Donna was unpredictable when it came to high emotional situations. To Darin's relief, her eyes started to well up too.

"I am sorry Darin. The therapist said that you needed extra care and support, and that's what I did. I didn't want to lose you too," Donna confessed, with relaxed shoulders and freely flowing tears. "After that girl on the slide almost died and the state got involved, I became terrified that I would let you and your mother down. I suppose I just got used to keeping our world small," Donna said, fully crying.

She got herself together a bit and told Darin that she was going to stop at the park. She did not want to drive while crying because it was dangerous. Darin held back from saying anything more. He did not want to upset her. If she was willing to talk, he could wait. Donna pulled into a park near their house. The same place that Darin used to go as a kid and where he met Joshua. She turned the car off and rolled her window down a bit.

After a few deep breaths, she spoke again. "I loved your mom, my sister. I had to learn to love you. I never wanted kids. I don't say that to hurt you, it's just the truth." Darin knew it was true, and her words didn't pierce him, but they still stung. "I made a promise, and I keep my promises. I am not very maternal, and I know it. Raising you was hard and scary. I felt like I had to protect you from everything.

Darin started to cry, but the tears were different. Something about them was life-giving and renewing. The truth can cleanse a body, even if it hurts. Darin looked out the window and back at Donna intermittently. He did not want to stare at her, but he did not want her to think that he was ignoring her either.

"I don't know how you're different exactly. The older I get I think that we are all different for better or worse. I was selfish and I was scared. I did not know what I was doing. All I knew was that if you were home, you were safe. If you were safe, I was a good mother and sister," Donna said with clarity and transparency.

Darin sat for a moment, absorbing the weight of this confession. His heart leaned toward rage. Then he thought about being in the same situation himself. He did not want kids yet; he knew nothing about them. It would be difficult to have a young child thrust on you with no warning or desire to raise one.

"I understand, Auntie," Darin said with compassion.

Donna erupted in tears that had been held back for years. The guilt, the fear, the shame, unleashing like a torrent. No longer held back by distractions or avoidance. She was a selfish and domineering parental figure that was just overwhelmed and underprepared. She did not maliciously keep Darin small; she was just afraid. She was just doing her best. Donna and Darin cried together and even held hands as they wept. Darin felt years of frustration melt away, and Donna seemed prettier and newer.

The people in the park kept walking and running. Families laughed and children played. Donna smiled, and her eyes brightened. Darin no longer felt like a child, or a slave kept as a hostage. He felt like his aunt's son, his mother's promise, his own man. He smiled too, and the warmth of the sun and the freshness of the air mingled into a moment of peace that he rested in. Everything was going to be all right, Darin thought.

"Jimmy is going to be hungry," Donna said after ample time to let the conversation be soaked in.

"I'm sorry for any way I've let you down. I will help you talk to Shannon. I still think she is too old for you, and I don't like the idea of my ... son starting out a marriage with baggage. If you don't think that matters, then I will talk to Miranda and find out if Shannon is available. Okay?"

Darin could tell that Donna was telling the truth. She had been overprotective, but she did have genuine concerns that had little to do with fearfulness. Darin agreed, and Donna smiled before starting the car. They left the park and drove home. Darin would never be a child again, and Donna had kept her promise to her sister, even if she struggled to do so.

Darin helped Donna carry in her bags, and Jimmy was sitting on the couch, clearly agitated by the disrupted routine.

"Where have you guys been?" Jimmy asked, showing a little aggression.

"I know I am late, but Darin and I had to have a talk. I'll fix you some sandwiches now," Donna told Jimmy, without responding to his agitation.

Jimmy nodded his head and could clearly see that there had been some emotional upheaval. He hugged Donna and went and sat back on his recliner. Darin headed for the basement stairs.

"Do you want some sandwiches, Darin?" Donna said, catching him before he disappeared.

"Yes, please," Darin said, with a warm smile.

"Okay, they will be ready soon," Donna said, as she returned to her work.

Darin went downstairs and looked at a picture of his mother. He did not know her, but he missed her dearly. She was lucky to have a sister promise to watch over her son, and he was glad that he was a part of this family, no matter how broken it had become by death. His mother had long black hair and fair skin. Her smile was wise and loving. He longed to go to her. She seemed infallible and almost magic.

The women in his life had abided by him, and he was no longer angry with Donna or his mother. They were, after all, just people, not saints, not blessed with infinite wisdom. Just little people, struggling against death and reality, equipped with whatever God had given them, no more and no less. Darin could see why his dad and Jimmy loved these sisters. He loved them too, and he was ready to forgive them. Darin kissed his fingers and then pressed them to the photograph of his mother.

As he headed back up the stairs, he passed by the folded flag that had been given to his mother after his father died. Something deep within him stirred. He could join the Army or Marines. He could be a man after all. He could serve his country and marry and support Shannon, all in one decisive move. The thought of joining the military had never occurred to him before. That day awoke something in him that would never be put back to sleep.

Darin climbed the steps to the living room, having made the decision that he would join the military. He would make his family proud, and he would finally be out in the world. Donna had made turkey and avocado sandwiches. She also served chopped strawberries to go with them. The cobbled family ate the food with little to no recognition that life was going to change for them all at once again.

"How was the service today?" Jimmy asked, after feeding his hunger.

"It was good. Why don't you come next week?" Donna answered.

Jimmy and Darin laughed.

"If it's good enough for you, honey, it's good enough for me, right Darin?" Jimmy said, chewing his last bite of the turkey sandwich. Darin laughed and agreed by nodding his head with a mouthful strawberries.

Chapter 26

Deciding which branch of the military to join was a daunting decision for Darin. He did not like the water, but the idea of debarking in exotic ports with a pocket full of cash was appealing. Then Darin remembered one of Marty's old pals, Greg, who was in the Navy. Greg always told stories of rough seas and cramped living conditions on breaks when he used to work with Marty.

"We were out at sea for months, and there had been so many sicknesses and conduct issues that the CO decided that we couldn't leave the port in Pattaya, Thailand," Greg said, bemused with only a brief pause.

"I had been getting stir-crazy, and the only thing keeping me going was the anticipation of getting drunk and meeting some girls," Greg laughed.

"That was it. I decided right then and there that I was only going to do one enlistment with the Navy." Marty and Darin laughed, and the men finished their coffee and continued working.

Darin did not want to be stuck on a ship with hundreds, if not thousands, of sick and bored guys for months on end with the possibility of never being allowed off the ship. The romantic notion of being a sailor that got tattoos in foreign lands while on furlough was dashed when Darin remembered Greg's stories. He would leave the Navy to other men. Darin's thoughts then turned to the Army.

His dad was in the Army. He fought and died in Vietnam. Darin saw his folded flag in a shadowbox every day. Darin did not want to die in combat, but he did want to fight and prove something to himself and others. He wanted to be tested; he wanted to know if he had courage or was a coward. Darin's mind was almost made up that he would join the Army, but he saw a commercial for the Marines.

It was a medieval setting. Most likely inferring the story of King Arthur. A knight rode into the castle and approached a king with a sword being charged with lightning. As the knight came nearer the king, the peasants looked on with admiration. The King knighted the man clad in armor after he dismounted from his horse. The narrator then said, "Once there were a few good men, men of adventure, men of courage, men who knew the meaning of honor. There still are, the Marines. We're looking for a few good men." The knight's gauntlet is replaced by a white glove when he receives the sword in his hand. Then the Marine salutes with the sword and is wearing a modern uniform that looks sharp and intimidating.

A tinge of guilt coursed through Darin as he realized that he wanted to be a Marine instead of a soldier. It wasn't that he didn't think that the Army was hard; his dad died fighting in the Army. It was the passion of being a warrior that inspired Darin. Fighting doesn't make a man a warrior. It was valor, duty, courage, and sacrifice that did. Adhering to a warrior's code, a fundamental change in identity, made a man into something else. Darin did not just want to fight; he wanted to be set apart.

The day after watching the commercial, Darin went to the Marine recruiter's office near his house. The building was ordered to perfection. The Marines were in uniform and looked powerful but composed. Violence seemed to emanate from their bearing, but it was contained by some invisible discipline. Darin was intimidated, but drawn. These were his people. This was his future.

Darin introduced himself to the Marine recruiters, and they bombarded him with questions.

"How old are you?"

"You got a record?"

"Why do you want to be a Marine?"

Darin answered as best as he could, and he almost told them that he wanted to be a warrior. But, instead, he said that he wanted to serve in the strongest fighting units.

The two men seemed satisfied with Darin's answers and handed him some paperwork to fill out.

"Go home and complete that packet. If you still want to be a Marine, call and set up an appointment for some tests," said a man with a perfect high and tight haircut.

Darin thought he would join the moment he walked into the office. He was relieved and disoriented by the dismissal.

"Ok, I'll fill it out and give a call. Can I get the phone number?" Darin asked.

"It's on my card in the packet," said the doppelganger to the Marine in the commercial Darin had watched.

"Oh, right, ok, I will do that," Darin answered with some visible shame for being stupid.

"One more thing: See that pull bar?" asked the jarhead.

Darin looked at the monstrosity. It was large and painted red.

"I see it," Darin answered.

"Get up on that bar and do as many pull-ups as you can," ordered the Marine.

Darin gulped. He was strong, but he never did pull-ups. He worked a lot and carried heavy bags and pushed unevenly loaded wheelbarrows. Darin did not want the men to think he was weak, but he really didn't know how to do a pull-up. Darin did not want them to know that he didn't know how to do pull-ups. He walked over to the bar, jumped up and grabbed it, while pulling himself up.

He kept pulling and counting to himself: One, two, three, four ... but the recruiter interrupted him.

"Not like that. You have to start each rep from a dead hang, and you can't kick or bicycle kick," the marine almost shouted.

"Hop off, I'll show you," said the clean-cut Devil Dog.

The man took off his top, folded it neatly, and revealed a powerful build adorned with strange tattoos on his arms. Then the Marine jumped on the bar, crossed his legs, and locked out his elbows in a complete dead hang. The Marine knocked out ten pull-ups in rapid succession but kept going. For some reason, Darin thought he would stop at ten, but he did not. The Marine passed twenty pull-ups in perfect form and continued to pull.

After thirty-four reps, the recruiter came off the bar, looking as fresh as he did before he did the exercise.

"That's how you do it, son," he said, putting his top back on.

Darin approached the bar and emulated the example he had just witnessed. After five perfect pull-ups, Darin started to kick and wiggle. The two men laughed, but Darin could tell it wasn't malicious. He did three more struggling reps before he was told to dismount the bar.

"Not bad, Darin, but you need to do better. Start practicing them now that you know the standard," ordered the sergeant.

Darin smiled. Not bad, he thought. The veiled compliment inspired Darin, and he nodded his head as he picked up the enlistment packet and reluctantly left the station. Darin walked to his car a little more erect; he was proud. He had never done proper pull-ups before, and he did five spontaneously. He would have been mortified if he could not have done any. He placed the packet on the passenger seat and admired it for a moment. Then he started his Pinto, and it cranked over on the first attempt.

The drive home was full of wonder and hope. He would be a warrior, he would get that sword, and he would be a fighting man. His thoughts turned to Shannon. He could ask her to marry him now. He would have the means to provide for her, and he had his own car. He could see her now, admiring his ability and commitment to the country. She would be proud to be his wife. They might even live on a beach somewhere.

Donna had set up a time for Darin and Shannon to meet. Apparently, Miranda, Shannon's mom, was not too keen on Darin. Donna said that he did not attend church very often, and he was a bit too quiet. Donna persisted that it was Shannon's choice, and that Darin and Shannon seemed to like each other. After some delay, Miranda conceded that Shannon would meet with Darin, but that she was just recently divorced.

Darin wished he would have just had the nerve to ask Shannon directly. But he knew that if Miranda was not involved in the process, it would go nowhere, even if Shannon did agree to have a date with him. For the first time, Darin realized that he did not even know Shannon. In his own mind they had conversations, and she would smile at him. But what if she was just being polite?

They had no real interactions. He would admire her, and she would smile back. They did exchange words, but it was nothing more than brief greetings and warm goodbyes. He felt like he knew her, that he loved her. In his own musings they were as good as man and wife. The internal world of passion is intoxicating, but desire for love is not the real thing, and it must be tested to be confirmed.

Darin came over to Miranda's house. Shannon had been living there since she got separated. The house was small and neat. There were many plants and figurines around the house. The appearance of the house made Darin feel annoyed. Why was it that women like Miranda always have figurines and wind chimes? The simple vanity bothered Darin because he knew that the type of woman that has an ornate yard would be the exact woman that wouldn't like a Marine.

Darin knocked at the door, and Shannon appeared with a warm smile that Darin experienced as kindred.

"Hey!" said Shannon, as soon as she opened the door.

Darin smiled a bit bashfully and said, "Hello."

Shannon giggled a bit at Darin's formality.

Shannon gestured for Darin to enter, and he did.

"Should I take my shoes off?" Darin said, beginning to bend down to untie them.

"Oh, no, don't worry about it," Shannon said

Darin stood and looked at her. He smiled and said, "Okay."

"Come on in and have a seat," Shannon said. "I am glad you finally asked to come over, Darin," as they both sat down on the floral-patterned loveseat.

Darin felt overwhelmed. The house smelled of potpourri, and Shannon radiated.

He had never told her how he felt, but it was clear that she liked him, too. He did not know what to say or where to begin.

"I am thinking about becoming a Marine. I went to the recruiter's office recently, and they gave me a packet to fill out," Darin blurted, relieved by having something to say.

Shannon smiled and paused. "Are you joining the Marines?"

"I think I am," Darin responded proudly.

"Does Donna know that?" Shannon asked in a serious tone.

"Well, not yet, but I don't need parental decisions anymore," Darin responded with some rigidity.

"Well, I know that, but she is not going to like it," Shannon said with a forced smile.

Everything was going wrong, Darin thought. He should have asked about her instead of blurting out that he was joining the Marines. Then he realized that Donna, Miranda, and possibly Shannon had a problem with the idea of a Christian wanting to be a Marine. Didn't they read the stories about David and Goliath? Didn't they remember that it was Joshua who carved out the promised land through warfare? His mind was going off the rails. He felt ashamed and almost angry.

He had thought that Shannon would be impressed and swoon over his decision. Instead, there was concealed judgement and slight expressions of being appalled. Darin had to rescue the situation.

He had not joined yet, and it would be true if he said he was only investigating the idea.

"I am thinking about it, but I'm looking at the Air Force, too," Darin said, lying, but adjacent to the truth. He was "thinking" about being a Marine, and he technically had not signed any documents.

The idea of joining the Air Force was not true. He knew that fighter pilots needed a college degree, and that was not for men like him. Some women like the idea of the Air Force. It's respectable and technical. The man gets all the benefits of military service without the perceived, if not real barbarity, of being a ground pounder. Especially ardent and pious Christian types. The Marines had nothing resembling a "walk of faith" to the Sunday brunch group of older ladies.

"Anyway, I am just thinking about it all. What are you up to these days?" Darin wanted to redirect the attention off himself.

"Well, I have started getting my associate's degree in dental hygiene. It's harder than I thought, but it's a good career that I can always fall back on," Shannon said proudly.

"That sounds pretty good. Having a degree is something to be proud of," Darin added.

"My mom said as long as I am working on improving myself, I can stay with her," Shannon continued. "It sucks, moving back home after you've already moved out. But I am grateful that she let me come back," Shannon said, losing a bit of her shine.

"How long have you been living with your mom?" asked Darin.

"About six months now, and I can't wait to get back on my feet. Do you want some coffee?" Shannon asked while standing up, ending the topic in a natural manner.

"Yes, please," Darin said.

"Cream and sugar?" Shannon added with a grin, teasing Darin a bit.

"Haha, no thanks, just black," Darin answered, concealing embarrassment about the time when he almost brought the gallon jug of milk to Shannon when she wanted a creamer.

Dimly, Darin began to become aware that he was at a crossroads. He had longed to be closer to Shannon. She was beautiful, alluring and mysterious from afar. As Darin sat at the table with Shannon in her mother's house, it occurred to him that who he wanted to be might cut him off from who he was. If he would have told Shannon that he was joining the Air Force, everyone would have been happy for him. However, the fact that a powerful subterranean urge for action dwelled within him was not something the women in his world were going to understand or be proud of.

"Is the school good?" Darin asked quickly, worried that he had been silent for too long.

"Yeah, I mean it's hard, but it's good," Shannon answered, reassuring him that she was still engaged in the conversation.

"Do you think that you will live with your mom until you finish your degree?" Darin asked, boldly cutting to the quick.

Shannon's smile dimmed a bit. Perhaps she was looking for a lighthearted get-to-know-you conversation. Darin felt pressure and needed to know if Shannon felt the same as he did about the idea of a relationship.

"I don't know, Darin. Divorce is hard, and I am just trying to get through it. Listen, I don't really want to talk about my situation.

I just want to get to know you a bit and have some coffee," Shannon announced.

Darin wanted to tell her that he wanted to marry her, for her to follow him on his journey as a Marine, wherever that took him. There was a chasm between his burnings and reality. Truth was, he didn't really know Shannon. Maybe Donna was right about her. He wanted to prove that his love for her would surmount any obstacles, but Shannon's immediate reaction to Darin's expressed desire of being a Marine had put him off balance.

Shannon was barely hanging on. She had failed and returned. Darin was just about to launch. He was headed up the mountain, and she was headed down to seek shelter. It was deeply disappointing for Darin to discover that his bubbling potential was not attractive to Shannon. The only thing he had to offer her was his future. He had no money, no accomplishments, and no proven experience except in manual labor.

Something snapped in Darin. He finished his coffee and started to squirm.

"Do you want some more coffee?" Shannon asked

"No, thank you," Darin replied.

A spell had been broken; an illusion had been smashed. Shannon was beautiful and would make someone a good wife. She would not be his wife. He wanted to be a warrior, and she wanted to nestle and exist in safety and predictability. Darin thought that when he told her his plans she would light up and swoon. But she didn't, and he almost resented her for it.

Love was dashed like morning fog at sunrise. He did not love Shannon, he just thought she was attractive. Reality and fantasy must merge or remain separate, Darin couldn't overlook the fact that she was unimpressed with his future desires.

They continued small talk for some time. Darin's thoughts drifted. He managed to be polite and stay engaged, but it was painful to observe a passion die while experiencing a meeting he had been longing for.

Miranda came into the living room area, broadcasting to the young courter that his time was nearing its end. Darin was relieved. It was almost unbearable to manage his feelings, be present and stay curious when he already knew the truth. If he wanted to be a Marine, Shannon was not interested in him. She wanted a dentist, an accountant, anything but a war fighter. Darin wanted nothing to do with repetitious safety and predictability; he wanted adventure and challenge.

Shannon smiled at Darin. It was clear that she hadn't picked up on his internal struggle. With her eyes she suggested that they go outside. Darin smiled and stood.

"Hey, Mom, I am going to walk Darin out," Shannon said in a calm and respectable tone.

"Yes, yes, we must get started with muffins," Miranda said, reminding Shannon of her commitment to the church breakfast they had agreed to support with baked goods.

"Yeah! I'll be just a moment," Shannon replied.

Miranda said nothing and bustled around the kitchen clearly agitated.

Darin and Shannon walked outside. The sun hit Darin's face, and he felt better. Being outside gave him a sense of freedom that he needed often. Cluttered houses and conversational expectations felt like wearing a turtleneck that was too small. He just wanted to stretch the neck and breathe, to escape the feeling of being suffocated.

"Darin, I saw that you were a bit dismayed by my reaction to you wanting to join the Marines. Listen, I think you're a handsome guy, but you're young. I felt like it would be nice to spend some time with you," Shannon began.

"I don't know if I'm going to join the Marines for certain," Darin protested.

Shannon smiled and reached out for his hand. Darin received her hand and felt electricity course through him the instant their hands touched.

"I could tell that you were disappointed, Darin," Shannon said warmly. "Don't let anyone for any reason pull you away from who you want to be. That's what my ex did to me, and now I'm living with my mom and starting over," Shannon added.

Darin began blushing. A mix of lust, recognition, and rejection congregated and left him gridlocked. He managed to rub her hand with his thumb but was tongue-tied. Shannon tilted her hand and invited him to be more present with her searching eyes. "If you want to be a Marine, then you should do that. People are going to tell you your whole life what is right and what is wrong. Just because something is true for someone else, doesn't mean it's true for you. I'm a bit older than you, and I don't want to be a military wife. I want to stay here in Portland and get my degree. That doesn't mean that your desire is wrong; it just means that I'm not the girl for you," Shannon said, grabbing Darin's hand firmer as she spoke.

Darin's eyes betrayed him, and they started to fill with tears. He fought them back and locked them in the same room where his dead parents were stored. Shannon beamed with love and understanding, and she firmly, and with gentleness, continued:

"I think you should go and be a Marine. You are too young for me anyway, but I do think you are handsome. Don't put so much pressure on yourself. You're a young guy with your whole life ahead of you".

Darin stood dumbfounded. Now he was drawn to her all over again, but it was different. She had rejected and blessed him in the way that only a good woman with compassion could do.

"I'll see you at church?"

"Yes..." Darin answered.

"Can I have a hug?" Shannon said, as she extended her arms in invitation.

Darin opened his arms, and they embraced. Her breasts pressed against his chest, and he became lost in the smell of her hair. He forgot himself and became intoxicated. Shannon broke the infusing connection first, and Darin surrendered his embrace.

"I'll see you Sunday," Shannon said, as she left Darin in his Pinto.

* * *

Darin was sitting alone in his barracks room. He couldn't remember the last time he had been by himself. The room was immaculate and barren except for spartan furniture. Sitting in his chair, he ran his hand over his fresh high and tight haircut. It was Friday evening, and his fire team was already out drinking. He rarely went out with them, not because he wasn't invited but because he feared the consequences of intoxication and belligerence.

He was alone, but not adrift. His thoughts often turned to Shannon, who married soon after he departed for boot camp. Did he make the right decision? He did not know, but he knew that he couldn't live for someone else's comfort ever again. It saddened him that he could not share his experiences with Shannon, but he was glad that she found a man that was kind and predictable. Over the last year he had done well in the Marine Corps, maxing out his PFT while obtaining an expert badge for marksmanship.

He belonged. He was not loved in a way that most would ever understand, but he was embraced and guided by the Corps in a way that was more than the love of family could offer. Darin had to decide between a woman and a future; he chose the latter, but not without moments of deep regret and unrequited longing. Such was the lot for the men in this world that want to go to the brink, to the edge of possibilities.

Donna came around, and she let him go, with her blessing, once she realized that Darin was going to join with or without her approval. The dynamic changed between them after he signed the enlistment papers. She stopped seeming like a mother and more like an aunt. She was his guardian, and he loved her. But she was not his mother, and she had no idea how to help Darin become a man. He had to break free; he had to sever the bonds which made him small and limited his ability to test himself.

He sat in his chair, still wearing his bottoms and boots. There was no point in immediately stripping off his uniform like many of his pals were in the habit of doing. Taking off his uniform didn't change the fact that he belonged to Uncle Sam twenty-four-seven. When he was in-processing, he was asked what religion he was. He told them that he was a Christian. The first time in his life that he declared his faith was when the Marines needed to know in case he died.

Darin did not really think of himself as a religious person until he had to come to terms with how he wanted to be buried and remembered. Death or even the hard reality of accepting its inevitability, has a way of making men choose. All thoughts become clearer, and games end when death is the consequence or the fact that must be acknowledged. His issued dog tags had CHRISTIAN embossed on them for religious preference.

God would understand even if Donna would not. He made this world; He made the kind of men that wanted to be war fighters. Black and white thinking was for women and children or the men that are never tested. The real world is grey and fraught with decisions between bad and worse. Only the brave are entitled to endure the complexity of God's design in the face of death. Darin was proud that he had enlisted. He longed for the love of a woman, but not at the expense of the pursuit of his purpose.

It started to rain while Darin was ruminating. He got up and looked out the window. Puddles formed where drains were obstructed. The people outside in the downpour maintained their military bearing and walked as if it wasn't raining at all. Darin smiled as he watched his fellow Marines carry on in the same manner, no matter what the heavens threw at them. With men like this in the world, it's no wonder how nations are forged.

Darin went to the bathroom to splash water on his face. His eyes looked foreign. He was frightened by his own image. He had a ruthlessness in him that was contained by discipline and, sometimes, luck. He felt safe and contained in the barracks. When he was in the world, he felt like a bomb that could go off at any moment. In the military, his internal energy and nature could be channeled, directed, and tempered. The warmth of a woman's love would have to wait. Darin un-bloused his bottoms and took off his boots. Then he laid on his perfectly made bunk and closed his eyes.

* * *

ABOUT THE AUTHOR

Magnus Johnson served as a Green Beret and received a Bronze Star during his time in the United States Army. After returning home, he co-founded Mission 22 and spent more than a decade listening to veterans and their families share the kinds of stories most people keep to themselves. Those conversations, along with his own experience, shaped his belief that men grow stronger when they learn how to help themselves and when they are given a clear path forward on how to do so.

In 2019, Magnus created the Recovery + Resiliency Program, drawing from behavioral studies, warrior psychology, and years of direct work with veterans. The same values that guide that program appear throughout The Men We Make. Identity, fatherhood, courage, loyalty, and the quiet choices that shape a man are themes he has seen lived out again and again.

Magnus also co-founded SALT for POTS, a program that supports individuals living with POTS and Long COVID. He holds a Master in Human Services Counseling and a Bachelor's degree in Social and Behavioral Studies as well as Board Certified Mental Health Coach.

He lives in Oregon with his wife, Sara, and their children. When he is not writing or working with veterans, he is usually hiking, running, training, or developing the next project meant to help someone find their footing again.